THE OTHER SIDE

AND FOUR OTHER STORIES

Milo McGivern

with illustrations by Yuliya Somina

Troubador Publishing Ltd
Unit E2 Airfield Business Park
Harrison Road, Market Harborough
Leicestershire LE16 7UL
Tel: 0116 279 2299
Email: books@troubador.co.uk
Web: www.troubador.co.uk/matador

ISBN 978 1805140 733

British Library Cataloguing in Publication Data.
A catalogue record for this book is available from the British Library.

Printed by TJ Books Limited, Padstow, UK
Typeset in 12pt Minion Pro by Troubador Publishing Ltd, Leicester, UK

Matador is an imprint of Troubador Publishing Ltd

MIX
Paper from
responsible sources
FSC® C013056

To Thomas 'Fats' Waller, Billie Holiday and JJ Cale. Truly inspirational musicians whose work I have enjoyed over many years.

TALES

HOW TO FIND THE LOCATION OF THE ISLAND OF ANIMAUX

Using Google Maps, type the island location included at the start of each story into the search field (for example, 36.5N 25.5E – remember to put a space between the two coordinates). When you click the search button, you will be taken to the relevant place on the map. Zoom out until you can see what part of the world Animaux is close to. In this case, it's off the island of Santorini. But be quick, as the island is moving all the time!

ONE

THE OTHER SIDE

Island of Animaux location:

- » latitude 49.93° north
- » longitude 6.25° west

Scene One – A Dark Place

Aubrey the Turkey had been awake all night. He hadn't dared to sleep. And now he was trying as hard as possible not to make a sound. Because in the darkness that smothered him, like a gigantic, suffocating blanket, he could hear dreadful noises – scratching and scraping sounds, shrill cries and sudden angry words in a language he didn't understand. And as he huddled there, his back pressed against a cold stone wall, his cape wrapped tightly around him and his top hat firmly pulled down, his knees hunched up under his chin, unknown and unwelcome things rustled in the darkness and occasionally and without warning brushed against him. He felt desperately alone and so afraid.

Where was he? WHERE WAS HE?

He certainly wasn't in the Cabinet of Esvaniss any more. Once again Aubrey analysed what had happened – from the moment he had stepped into the cabinet many hours before, to where he was now. He had been very confident. It was a simple trick. He would say the disappearing spell, wait a few moments and then say the reappearing spell. And then he would open the cabinet door and step out, no doubt to warm applause from Clifford and Walli.

But something unexpected had happened. As soon as Aubrey had said the disappearing spell, he had started to feel incredibly dizzy and had felt a tingling all over his body, as if he was receiving a mild electric shock. This had completely distracted the turkey from saying the reappearing spell. The funny feeling had lasted about ten seconds, and he put it down to his excitement that, after all the failed tricks he had tried earlier that evening, this one was actually going to work.

Feeling better, Aubrey cleared his throat and said the reappearing spell. Luckily he remembered it, as it was too dark in the cabinet to read from the book of spells that he was clutching in his right wing.

Having chanted the reappearing spell, very pleased at how clearly he pronounced every word,

Aubrey reached out for the cabinet door. But it wasn't there. There was just empty space. He cursed quietly, thinking that he must have moved around when he felt dizzy. He needed to leave the cabinet quickly, otherwise Clifford and Walli might think that he had messed up this trick as well.

Aubrey put the book of spells in the inner pocket of his cloak and began to grope around with both wings. But still he couldn't find the door. Or any of the sides of the cabinet. This frustrated him enormously. Being a lazy bird, and also now fed up with the trick, he called out to his friends to open the cabinet door for him. But the door didn't open, nor did they reply. He called again, then once more, then many times. Each time his voice became more desperate. Aubrey continued to reach out with his wings, stumbling this way and that in the dark. Why hadn't he found some part of the cabinet, given that it wasn't very big inside?

And why hadn't Clifford and Walli opened the door? Clifford did like to play tricks, but surely Walli would have opened the door – especially if she had heard the tearful Aubrey say, "Please let me out, I'm frightened" after he had searched, to no avail, for what seemed like hours.

As he floundered about, Aubrey noticed that he was no longer walking on the cold, wooden floor of the cabinet, but on something that was springy and that had occasional sharp bits that made him hop in pain when he trod on them with his bare feet.

With his mind still focused on when he would stand on the next spiky bit, and as he continued to blindly lurch about, Aubrey walked straight into a stone wall. He had no idea it was there, and so he hit it at speed, taking a nasty bang on his beak and left knee. Pausing a few seconds to rub his damaged beak and to utter a few more curses, Aubrey felt along the wall for a little while. But unable to find where it began or ended, he slumped down, his back to it.

For the umpteenth time, and this time more loudly than before, he called out the reappearing spell, although with no real hope that it would make any difference.

"Mysterious cabinet
Hear me clear,
Make this creature
Reappear."

This time his shouting *did* make a difference. But not the one he hoped for. The noise seemed to attract the attention of … something that was out there, somewhere in the dark. And whatever the 'something' was, it sounded angry.

And this was why he hadn't slept all night. Perhaps he had dozed for a few minutes, but surely for no longer. By this point, poor Aubrey was too tired to remember.

Aubrey was beginning to despair that he would never see daylight again when, as if by divine intervention, dawn began to appear.

As the darkness receded, Aubrey got a clearer idea of where he was. He seemed to be in a large room. As it grew lighter, he could see that it was actually a barn. It was rectangular and he was sitting near one of the corners on a short side, looking down the length of the building. The walls were made not of stone but of breeze block and there were quite a few windows through which the dawn light shone, but the windows were very high up on the walls. The barn had a vaulted metal roof, with rafters just below it.

As the light continued to improve, he could see more and more. The floor of the barn was covered with straw – this was the springy, spiky stuff he had been walking on. And there were a number of low metal bins or troughs placed around the barn. The ones closest to him were filled with grain or water. He assumed all the other ones were as well.

The scratching, squawking noise that Aubrey had heard earlier was still present. And as he peered down the barn he found out, to his horror, where it was coming from. There in the distance, across the entire width of the building, was a seething, noisy white mass about one metre tall. It was undulating across its entire length, like some kind of gigantic maggot. Aubrey couldn't believe what he was seeing. What type of terrible monster was this? He had never seen anything like it on Animaux before!

And then, in a truly heart-stopping moment for the turkey, the white mass suddenly started to head in Aubrey's direction, rolling across the floor like a ghastly pale tsunami.

On and on it came, boiling and seething, the awful noise getting louder and more threatening.

Aubrey sat watching it, straitjacketed by terror and unable to move a muscle. He had never been so frightened before, not even when he had been dangling over the terrible, open mouth of the Black Skullanthemum. He began to hyperventilate. His ears ringing – caused by his thundering heart rate – Aubrey closed his eyes and prepared for his end.

The white mass was soon upon him. He was engulfed, and Aubrey once again felt things brushing against him, like he had in the darkness the night before. But the things seemed soft and gentle, not sharp or threatening. And the awful squawking had changed to a low murmur … a murmur that had a strangely familiar quality to it.

After what felt like an eternity but in reality was only about twenty seconds, Aubrey nervously opened his eyes. And he got the biggest surprise of his life. Rather than looking at a giant maggot, Aubrey found that he was surrounded by countless faces. Faces with eyes that were all staring at him. Faces attached to heads, attached to necks, attached to plump bodies covered with white feathers, each of which stood on a pair of bare legs.

Turkeys. Lots of turkeys.

Aubrey was surrounded by perhaps two hundred turkeys.

He had never seen so many before, and he studied them as best he could. They looked almost the same as him; the only apparent difference was the colour of their feathers.

The turkeys didn't seem to be threatening, so Aubrey decided to stand up. As he rose to his full height, he noticed that he was much taller than them. This gave him a surge of confidence, and he decided to make first contact with the alien fowl.

"Greetings, my fellow turkeys. My name is Aubrey.

I am from the little house at the end of Fluffy Cloud Lane and I come in peace."

"Gobble, gobble," said the turkey immediately in front of him.

"Gobble, gobble," said the one to its side.

"Gobble, gobble?" repeated Aubrey. This was not what he had expected to hear. "Turkeys, who is your leader? Take me to them."

"Gobble, gobble," said a turkey on the far left.

"Gobble, gobble," said a turkey on the far right.

And then suddenly, as if all the individual turkeys were controlled by a single brain, they seemed to lose interest in him and began to quickly move away, in a large group, back down the barn. As they went, Aubrey noticed that each had a red tag on its leg, and on each tag was a letter followed by a number. The number on each tag was unique.

SCENE TWO – THE PEOPLE-CREATURES.
AND A SALAMANDER

Perhaps the turkeys had heard something, perhaps something always happened at this time of day, or perhaps this was just another tidal motion or random walk by a not-very-clever group of creatures, but they seemed determined to return to the opposite end of the barn as soon as possible.

As soon as they had reached their destination, a small door set within a larger door at the end of the barn opened and two strange creatures came in. They walked on two legs and had two arms hanging from their sides. One had short dark hair on its head and the other had long hair at the sides of its head, tied in a ponytail at the back; the top of its head was bald.

They were dressed in blue overalls and calf-length rubber boots. Both carried brooms, and one carried a bucket. The turkeys seemed pleased to see them, gobbling excitedly as the strange creatures, after slamming the door shut, moved between them.

The bucket-less strange creature went through a door into a small office at the far end of the barn and turned the light on.

The other strange, partly bald creature walked around the top half of the barn, checking the contents of the food troughs. It refilled each one as necessary, from the grain it had in its bucket. Apparently, all the water troughs were OK so it didn't refill them.

Its work seemingly at an end, the strange creature then looked at the turkeys. Putting down the bucket and broom, it laughed, unkindly kicked out at a few turkeys that had come too close, then started to make a gobbling sound, at the same time flapping its arms like the turkeys flapped their wings. This seemed to please the strange creature, and it laughed even louder.

And then Aubrey's blood turned to ice and he was frozen to the spot. The strange creature had noticed him, and began to walk in his direction. As it neared Aubrey the strange creature yelled out to the other one. "Oi, Phil – look at the one at the back of the barn. What's it wearing? Hey, some silly so-and-so has put a cape and a top hat on it! Was it you?"

The strange creature called Phil had come out of the office to see what all the fuss was about. "Of course not, Mick! Why would I do that? It was probably Karolina yesterday. She's always having a laugh."

The strange creature called Mick reached Aubrey and picked the turkey up. It held him so that their faces were opposite each other. The two creatures regarded each other silently. Aubrey noticed that the strange creature had plaque-encrusted yellow teeth and foul breath, which reminded him of Rick Rat. For some reason, the turkey found this strangely comforting.

Realising that one of them needed to break the ice, Aubrey decided to introduce himself.

"Good morning, strange creature Mick. I am pleased to meet you. My name is Aubrey the Turkey. Would you mind telling me what kind of creature you are, and where I am?"

But the strange creature did not reply. It continued to regard Aubrey with interest. Aubrey tried again.

"I arrived last night, although I'm not sure how. I'm rather hungry and thirsty. I see there is grain and water in the troughs, but I'm not very keen on those. Would it be possible to order a cheese sandwich and some apple juice?"

The strange creature called Mick kept looking at him, although this time it once again yelled to the other one.

"This one makes a different gobbling noise to the others. Why's that, then? And it's much fatter – it weighs half a tonne. Greedy bird – it's obviously been scoffing too much grain."

With that, the strange creature removed Aubrey's hat, tore off his cape and threw him roughly onto the floor. The turkey landed painfully on his left side.

"It's a different colour as well," said Mick, stuffing the cape inside the upturned top hat. "Look – its feathers are dark. This must be one of Karolina's jokes. I'm going to have a word with her."

Mick walked back down the barn holding the hat, pausing briefly to collect the bucket and broom. Walking on, Mick threw Aubrey's top hat and cape into the small office, closed the door, and then both it and the other strange creature exited the barn, leaving Aubrey all alone in a sea of inarticulate turkeys.

The now-aching Aubrey dragged himself over to the barn wall and sank down, so that his back was once again against it. He stared ahead and pondered his situation. So this was it! This was to be his life from now on. This was all he could look forward to. Stuck in this barn with lots of other turkeys, none of whom he could understand. With nothing decent to eat or drink. And probably with more unwelcome visits from the strange creatures. Aubrey would never return to his house. Or see his family and friends. He knew that he was sometimes not the nicest turkey, but he simply couldn't imagine what awful thing he had done to deserve this. Tears of unhappiness welled in his eyes as he mournfully reflected on his lot.

Suddenly a voice called out.

"Hello, turkey. Welcome to the farm."

The voice caught Aubrey completely by surprise. He looked around. The rest of the turkeys were still gathered at the far end of the barn, gobbling and pecking and jostling each other and scraping the ground with their claws. So the voice couldn't have come from one of them. And anyway, they couldn't speak.

"Up here," came the voice again. "I'm on a rafter."

Aubrey looked up. Straining his eyes, he looked at the rafters closest to him. At first he couldn't see anything, but then he noticed a small creature staring down at him. It was lizard-like, black and, he estimated, about twenty centimetres long.

"Hold on, I'm coming down," it said. Immediately the creature ran, upside down, along the rafter towards the wall, then straight down the wall, head-first. Aubrey watched it in astonishment and fascination, noticing that it had many yellowish-orange spots on its back and wondering how it managed to keep its grip.

Just before it reached the bottom of the wall, the creature stopped. It opened its mouth, stuck out a very long tongue, and proceeded to lick its eyes, one after the other. Then it put its tongue back in its mouth and continued its journey down the wall. At the bottom, the creature jumped onto the straw then stood upright, walking towards Aubrey on its hind legs and extending its right front leg to shake the turkey's wing.

"Hi there," it said. "Let me introduce myself. My name's Solomon. But you can call me Sol for short."

Aubrey shook the creature's leg, noting that its small, bony toes were dry although the rest of its body glistened. "And my name is Aubrey. Aubrey the Turkey."

"Nice to meet you, Aubrey. And I'd already worked out what you are," replied Sol with a wry smile. "Did you arrive last night? I must have been asleep when you turned up. Did one of the people-creatures bring you in? And why did they put that cape and top hat on you? What a silly thing for them to do."

"I'm not sure when I arrived," reflected Aubrey. "It was certainly very dark when I did."

"It's amazing," continued Sol. "I've been here for quite a while, but this is the first time I've been able to have a discussion with another creature. I heard you talking to the other turkeys and the people-creatures, but of course they didn't understand what you were saying."

"So those two-legged things were people-creatures?" asked Aubrey. "I've heard about them from friends, and read things about them on the Turkeynet, but that's the first time I've seen them in real life. They're much bigger and stronger than I imagined. And they're also not very friendly – it really hurt when that one grabbed me and pulled my cape off. And there was absolutely no need for it to throw me on the ground afterwards like it did."

"You're going to need to get used to it," replied Sol. "In my experience, the male people-creatures are the roughest. It was one of them that grabbed you. Whenever they see me they throw things at me, like brooms or buckets or whatever they can lay their hands on. I actually think they're trying to squash me – but why would they want to do that? The female people-creatures are generally nicer, although you also get some bad ones of that type."

"How can you tell which one is male and which one is female?" asked Aubrey, keen to find out more.

"The male ones tend to have deeper voices and sometimes hair on their faces. And they tend to be a bit taller than the female ones. The females sometimes have longer hair on their heads … and their bodies are different shapes."

"And do they always wear clothes?" Aubrey probed. "Where I come from, most of the creatures make do with their fur or feathers or scales. Although I always like to wear some clothes, to show how clever and superior I am."

"I haven't seen them without their clothes," said Sol. "Perhaps they wear them for protection, or to keep out the cold. By the way, Aubrey, it's what you say and what you do that is the measure of how clever you are, not what you wear. And in this barn all the creatures are equal – you included. Thinking you are superior could get you into big problems, especially with the people-creatures, who are actually pretty intelligent."

Aubrey was quiet for a while, aware that Sol had just chastised him. Then he spoke up. "I could understand everything the people-creatures were saying. Why couldn't they understand me?"

"A very good question, Aubrey, but unfortunately I don't know the answer," replied Sol. "Perhaps there's a switch in their brain that isn't turned on. I can understand them as well. But I've never been able to understand what the turkeys in here are saying – apart from you."

Aubrey looked down the barn at all the other turkeys. They were still huddled together, continuing to peck at whatever was peckable. They had lost all interest in him.

"The turkeys are the same type of creature as me. OK, their feathers are different colours, but that shouldn't stop us being able to understand each other, should it?"

Sol had a ready answer. "I think they *are* speaking, in their own way. I call it Turkese. It's a very primitive language. In the three years I've been here, I've tried on many occasions to teach them to speak like us."

"Are they slow learners, then?" asked Aubrey. "They didn't make a single sound that I could understand. It was just an awful cacophony."

Sol gave a weary sigh. "I've had limited success. The turkeys don't have names, but the people-creatures put numbered tags on their legs – I think, to keep track of them. A year ago, I managed to teach turkey number F217 the alphabet and to say a few simple words. But I always face the same problem."

"That you're not a very good teacher?"

Sol looked quite offended by the remark, and for a few seconds his spots glowed more brightly than usual. But he chose not to rise to Aubrey's barbed comment. "Not at all. It's because the turkeys keep changing, so I never have enough time to teach them properly."

"What do you mean, 'keep changing'? How can they change when they are all locked in this barn?"

"It happens about four times a year. The people-creatures come and take them all away. Then they bring in some younger ones, they get bigger over the next few months, and then the people-creatures take them away again. It's currently summer, so there aren't too many turkeys here at the moment. But when it gets to winter the barn will be almost completely full."

Aubrey drank it all in, but was still thirsty for more answers. "Where do the turkeys go? Where do the people-creatures take them?"

"I'm not sure. They get shooed out through the big door at the end of the barn, loaded onto lorries and driven away. They never come back, including number F217. Which was a pity, because I had taught her to say almost a whole sentence. In the winter the people-creatures celebrate something called Christmas, and I think the turkeys help them in some way."

"When will the turkeys that are here now be taken by the people-creatures?" asked Aubrey, suddenly nervous in case he was taken too.

"Not for a few weeks. Things should be quiet for a while."

Suddenly all the turkeys started to make a terrific, frightened gobbling noise. Perhaps they had seen a rat.

"*Relatively* quiet," Sol corrected himself.

The two creatures sat patiently and waited for the turkeys to calm down.

"Back to my earlier questions, Aubrey. I assume that the people-creatures brought you in. But why did they put that cape and top hat on you?"

"They didn't, and they didn't," replied Aubrey. "I got here all on my own."

"Now it's my turn not to understand," said Sol. "What do you mean?"

"It's a long story," began Aubrey. "But to

summarise, I was at home doing a magic show. That's why I was wearing the cape and the top hat. It was my costume for my role as Aubrey the Extraordinary."

"OK – got it so far. What happened next?"

"Something went wrong with one of my tricks. It was my last one – the disappearing trick. I climbed into a special cabinet, read a few words that I'd learnt from a magic book, and then disappeared. I wasn't actually supposed to disappear. I wasn't supposed to go anywhere. But the next thing I know, I've ended up here and it's the middle of the night. I've said the reappearing spell lots of times but it hasn't worked. So it looks like I'm stuck."

Sol was staring at Aubrey, his mouth wide open and a look of horror on his little lizard face.

"What's wrong, Sol?" asked Aubrey, concerned at the strange face the lizard was pulling. "I didn't mean to shock you. I know it sounds like an odd story, but I promise that it's true."

Sol finally regained the power of speech. "I don't believe it! I don't believe it!" he blurted.

"What's wrong? What don't you believe?"

"You're from the Island of Animaux, aren't you, Aubrey?"

"Yes, I am! But how did you know that?"

"As I said earlier, I've been here for quite a while. But about three years ago, I was on Animaux. I used to live there. I'd been doing a lot of magic shows around the island and my last dates were at the Grand Theatre in Cedilla on Sea. I decided to put something new into my act, as I'd been on the road for quite a while and was getting a bit bored with the show."

"You're not the Great Salamander, are you?" asked Aubrey, almost too excited to get the words out.

"I used to be," replied Sol. He looked thoughtful for a few seconds. Clearly, what Aubrey had said meant a lot to him.

"Wow – no one has called me that for years. It was so long ago. Those were the days!"

"So what happened at the Grand Theatre? I heard that you did the disappearing trick and vanished, just like I did."

"There was an old wardrobe in my dressing room at the Grand. It was made of lovely black wood. I thought I might ask the theatre management to let me have it when I had finished my performances. But then I had a better idea. I decided to use the wardrobe as a prop for my final show. I thought it would be neat if I used it as a disappearing cabinet. You know – I get in, close the door, say some words, and the cabinet vanishes. The audience would go wild – where has it gone? Then I say the reappearing spell, the cabinet returns and I step out to take the inevitable wild applause."

"OK, Sol – all very clear so far."

"Making the cabinet really disappear was going to be a big problem. I didn't want to use smoke and a trapdoor in the stage floor. I wanted the trick to be real."

"How did you do that?"

"Thanks to the Weird Sisters. Have you heard of them?"

"Yes, but they're just make-believe, aren't they?"

"No, they really exist. Anyway, on the morning before my final show I travelled up from Cedilla on Sea and visited them in their cave, to ask for a disappearing spell. I told them it had to involve the wardrobe and so on, and then they said some words and waved their paws and put the spell in a paper bag for me to take away. They also told me the words to the spell and I memorised them, meaning to write them in my book of spells when I got back to the theatre. It was all very expensive – the visit cost me ten tins of sardines, eight gold eagles and three of my spots. I wonder why they wanted the spots…"

"What happened next?" asked Aubrey.

"I got back to the theatre just in time, because my train from Wincot was delayed. Something to do with stick insects on the line. And so I was rushing and not paying attention properly. The show was due to start in fifteen minutes and I still needed to write the words of the disappearing and reappearing spells in my book, get changed, move the wardrobe from my dressing room to the stage, and apply the actual spell, which was still in the paper bag." Sol paused for breath. Aubrey silently urged him to carry on, desperate to hear what happened next.

"Anyway, I thought I'd got everything done. Then the curtain went up and my show started. All went really well – it was one of my best performances. The crowd's applause got louder and louder with each new trick, and I knew that my final trick, when I disappeared, would truly amaze them.

"Time flew by. Before I knew it, there was only the disappearing trick left. I gave it a big announcement, talking about the mysterious Cabinet of Esvaniss, a name I made up on the spot, and how I would be able to make it, and me, vanish. And then, to my horror, I realised that I had forgotten to empty the magic spell out of the paper bag the Weird Sisters had given me. I'd put the bag in the wardrobe before it was carried from my dressing room to the stage, but then I had been distracted by something, I can't remember what, and it had slipped my mind."

"What did you do?" asked Aubrey, absorbed by the story.

"I got the bag out, making a weak joke to the audience that it contained my supper. And then I couldn't remember what to do with the spell! Should I sprinkle it over the cabinet? Should I sprinkle it over me? The Weird Sisters had told me what to do but I obviously hadn't been listening properly, as I think they were removing my spots at the time. So I mentally tossed a coin in my mind. It came down on the side of Elizabeth Eagle's head and so I sprinkled the contents over my head. The crowd thought this was very funny and I got a big laugh. Then I climbed into the cabinet, said the disappearing spell – and landed here, in this barn. With no way of getting back to Animaux."

"No way of getting back?!" gasped Aubrey, horrified. "But you are the Great Salamander, the finest magician on the whole of Animaux. If you can't get back, what hope is there for me?"

"Aubrey, over the past three years I've had plenty of time to think about what happened that night at the Grand. And I've come to realise that I made two really big mistakes."

"What were they?" asked Aubrey, his head still spinning with the news that he would never be going home.

"The first was where I sprinkled the spell. I should have sprinkled it over the outside of the cabinet, not on me. The second was how I wrote down the words of the spell. In the version I wrote in my book and said on the night, the words were 'make this creature disappear'. What I *should* have said was 'make this cabinet disappear'."

"I'm not sure I follow," said Aubrey.

"The spell needed to apply to the cabinet, not the creature inside it. And the spell should have asked the cabinet to disappear, along with any creature inside it. And so both the cabinet and its contents should have vanished. Without the cabinet, there is no way of getting back to Animaux."

"But that doesn't make sense!" the turkey spluttered. "I didn't sprinkle any of the magic on me, yet I was still transported here."

"I suppose some of the magic I sprinkled on myself must have fallen on the cabinet floor. Obviously it still works, even though it's a few years old. You must have stepped in it when you entered the cabinet. You said the incorrect disappearing spell – and hey presto!"

"That's just great!" howled Aubrey, almost unable to believe his bad luck. But suddenly he thought he saw a way out of their predicament. "What about all the other spells in your book? I brought it with me – it's in a pocket in my cape! You can have it! You are the Great Salamander! Surely one of those spells can get us home?"

Sol shook his head. "Sorry, Aubrey, but all the spells in the book are rubbish. I made them up! Being a great magician is all about creating an illusion – making the audience believe you're doing something that actually isn't possible. A few fancy words, a little bit of mumbo-jumbo-it all adds to the effect."

"S-s-so, you're not a great magician?"

"I'm afraid not. My shows were full of fluff and bluff. Smoke and mirrors. The only true magic I ever tried was the disappearing trick – and look where that ended for both of us."

Sol looked at Aubrey. The turkey was clearly taking the news very badly.

"I'm really sorry, Aubrey. I would give anything for this not to have happened to you. Because of my silly trick, your life has been ruined. But here's the deal. I will do all I can to get us both back to Animaux, I promise you."

Aubrey gave Sol a little nod, although he doubted that either of them would ever see Animaux again. He decided to change the subject, to lighten his mood and to find out more about the here and now. "So where are we? What is this place?"

"It's called the Five Wards Turkey Farm. There's a sign on the roof outside the barn. It's also written on some stationery in the office down there."

Sol continued to explain. "I know we're not on Animaux – on the wall of the office there's a map including islands and places I've never heard of. But we seem to be near a place called Pelistry Bay on an island called St Mary's. That's in a group of islands called the Isles of Scilly. And the group is off the coast of a larger island called Great Britain. Where Great Britain is, I have no idea."

A bell rang deep in Aubrey's mind. "I wonder if this is similar to the place that Walli and Clifford came from, and Hughie, Rina and Washington," he muttered, thinking out loud. "They did say there was a world beyond Animaux – a world on the other side. Maybe we have both travelled to it."

The turkey thought a little bit more. "Wait a minute! If Walli and Clifford could travel to Animaux, why can't we? There must be a way back. But how did they get to Animaux? Remember, Aubrey! Remember! Ah – that's it! Walli ran into a tunnel, and Clifford was swimming before he also went into a hole."

Slowly, Aubrey was putting all the pieces of the puzzle together. "Sol, are there any holes or water nearby?"

"I don't know about holes, but there is water. In fact, rather a lot of it. I think we're quite close to the sea."

"How do you know we're close?" asked Aubrey. "Can you smell the salt air?"

"No. I've left the barn a few times, to explore. I never stay out for long, as I seem to be a target for the local cats, and the gulls. That's why I live up in the rafters – it's much safer there. But I do know there's a beach only a short distance from here. We could go there and see if getting in the water takes us back to Animaux?"

"Good thinking, Sol. But we need to organise a few things first. I'm a wise old bird, and my experience tells me you should always have a fallback plan, in case what you first try goes wrong. And since we're near the sea I think the fallback plan should be sending a message in a bottle. So if we're not successful getting back to Animaux, this time at least, we can throw a message in the sea and hope that it somehow gets back to our home."

"Great idea, Aubrey," said Sol, looking impressed at the turkey's logical thinking. "And I've got everything we need to send the message. The people-creatures sometimes give the turkeys medicine, and I've been keeping the empty bottles they throw away. I've got a few stored up on the rafters. And because I like art and drawing I took a notebook they kept in the office. I write and sketch in it when I get bored. We can tear some pages from that to write on."

"What about ink? We can't write a message without any ink."

Sol was two steps ahead of Aubrey. "I made some about six months ago, and I've still got plenty left. I put it in one of the old medicine bottles."

"How did you make it?"

"It was quite simple, really. I collected some soot from a fire that the people-creatures had started outside, and mixed it with water and with some gum arabic I made from plants that I found growing near the beach. It's good stuff, although do try not to get any on your feathers, as it won't wash off."

"Great!" gobbled Aubrey in high excitement. "Can you bring some paper and the ink down, and two empty medicine bottles? I need to start writing!"

"I usually use a bit of straw to write and draw with. It's not great, but it does the job," suggested Sol.

"I'm going to use the quill from one of my feathers," said Aubrey. "I think that it will add a nice, old-fashioned touch."

Sol scooted up the wall and quickly returned with the empty bottles, each with a worn label saying

'Galliform Bumblefoot Medicine'. He also had another bottle containing the ink and two sheets of paper. He was wearing a small wizard's hat.

"I used to wear this when I was performing. I couldn't leave it behind," he said with a smile.

Aubrey set to work writing the note. He pulled out a nice big feather, wincing a little as he did so. Then he skilfully shaped the featherless end into a nib. Pausing for a few seconds to think what he was going to write, he uncorked the bottle in which the ink was stored and wetted the nib with it. And then he began to write. The words flowed smoothly onto the page, only being interrupted when it was time to refill the nib with ink.

After about five minutes Aubrey had finished. He had put his heart into what he had written, and Sol noticed that the turkey had tears streaming down his cheeks as he blew on the words to dry the ink. Then he turned the paper over and wrote the following:

> *Dear finder,*
> *Please deliver this message to Clifford Platypus*
> *and Walli Hog. They live in the little house at*
> *the end of Fluffy Cloud Lane. Thank you.*

Aubrey blew on these words as well then rolled the paper up so that it would fit into one of the bottles, ensuring that the address he had written was on the outside of the roll. He removed the cork from the square bottle, pushed the message though the neck then firmly rammed the cork back in, ensuring it was watertight. The paper had unrolled slightly when it was inside the bottle, and Aubrey was pleased to see that the address was clearly visible through the thick greenish-brown glass, on the opposite side of the label.

Aubrey then started his second task. But instead of writing another note, he began to draw a map. A map of the Island of Animaux. The island where he was born and had lived all his life. The island that he loved more than he could find words to say. And as he wrote the names of the various towns on the map, more tears fell from his eyes and splashed onto the paper, causing the ink to run and smudge.

When he was finished, Aubrey didn't put an address or any other note on the reverse of the paper. Rather, he just rolled up the map and pushed it into the other empty bottle. He also pushed in the feather he had used to write with, as a keepsake for the finder. He then sealed the bottle in the same way he had sealed the first. This wasn't a message intended for anyone in particular; rather, it was a simple sketch drawn for posterity.

His work at an end, Aubrey turned to Sol. "Let's go," he said, sniffing. His eyes were red from crying.

The two creatures walked to the far end of the barn. The other turkeys paid them no attention. Aubrey and Sol paused briefly at the small office, so that Aubrey could recover his cape and top hat. He noticed that there was a computer on a table in the office. It looked newer than the one he had in his house, and he wondered if it would be as easy to use. But there was no time to find out. Returning to Animaux had to be his priority.

Scene Three – Freedom at Last?

The small door to the barn was only on the latch, rather than locked, so Aubrey had no problem opening it. With Sol sitting on his shoulder he carefully closed the door behind him, making sure that none of the other turkeys escaped.

Sol moved onto Aubrey's head as the turkey, squinting as he got used to the sunlight after the relative gloom in the barn, put on his cape. Sol returned to the turkey's shoulder as Aubrey donned his top hat.

With the two message bottles firmly inserted into one of the cape's inner pockets, since the other still contained the book of spells, Aubrey strode swiftly and purposefully towards the beach, with Sol whispering directions into his ear. As they moved along, the turkey kept half an eye open for people-creatures and Sol kept both eyes open for cats and gulls.

To their great relief, the journey to the beach was straightforward. The beach was sandy and unoccupied and the weather was gorgeous. The sun was warm, with only a light breeze, and Aubrey and Sol started to feel optimistic about their chances of getting back to Animaux. They still had no idea what they would do when they got to the shore, apart from Aubrey throwing the bottles into the sea. But both felt that things would take care of themselves and that everything would be all right.

Aubrey rushed down to the water's edge. He took the first bottle from the cape pocket and threw it as hard and as far as he could into the sea. The bottle landed with a splash, bobbed about for a while, then got caught by a strong current and was quickly carried away. Aubrey threw in the second bottle. Again it landed with a splash, but this time it evaded any currents and just bobbed gently about before slowly drifting further down the beach. Aubrey and Sol didn't notice that it had washed ashore about a hundred metres from them.

Now it was time to start the return journey to

Animaux. Aubrey took a few steps forward and dipped his foot into the water. It was ice cold and completely uninviting, even though it was a warm day.

Being a bird who always took the easy option, and who always avoided physical exertion when he had a chance to sit on his bottom, Aubrey walked backwards until his feet were on dry, warm sand. He sat down, Sol still on his shoulder.

"Any idea what we should do next?" he asked his amphibian friend.

"Sorry, Aubrey, but no. You're the one who knows creatures that have travelled from this place to Animaux. I was following your lead."

The two friends sat quietly for what felt like a long time, staring out to sea. Then Sol spoke.

"What's that over there?"

"What's what? Over where?" Aubrey replied, trying to see what the salamander was referring to.

"That bank of fog. Look – there, to the right. It wasn't there a few minutes ago."

Aubrey located the fog bank and both creatures studied it. It was about two kilometres offshore. Although it wasn't moving either left or right, the fog seemed to be swirling around. Sometimes it cleared enough to show a glimpse of land – perhaps an island – beyond it.

"Have you ever seen that when you've visited the beach in the past?" asked Aubrey.

"Well, I haven't been here that many times. But I've always looked out to sea and I can say with complete confidence that the fog has never been there before."

The friends continued to look at the fog, straining to see what was behind it. Then Aubrey leapt up and cried out. "Mount Verticus! That's Mount Verticus!"

"Aubrey – you're right!" shouted Sol. "I know we usually see it from the land-facing side, but that's definitely Mount Verticus. But what is the Island of Animaux doing here?"

"It's come for us, Sol, it has come for us! There's no time to lose – we've got to get across to it. But how?"

"How about swimming?" asked Sol.

"No, that won't work. The water is too cold, it's too far away, the currents look pretty dangerous, and anyway, I'm not a good swimmer. Are you?"

"No, I'm a rubbish one," replied Sol. "So what are we going to do? If it has just appeared out of nowhere, then it might disappear equally quickly."

"Think! THINK!" bellowed Aubrey, largely to himself, frantically trying to come up with a plan. And then the solution came to him. "I can fly there! Silly turkey, why didn't you think about that before?"

"Are you sure you can fly, Aubrey? The turkeys in the barn can't – at least, I've never seen them do it."

"Yes, no problem. I once flew all the way to the top of Blackrock. This will be a lot harder, but I'm sure I can do it. OK, I need something to stand on to take off from."

Sol looked around. "What about that low wooden fence just over there? It's got some posts along it. If we get on the wall then climb onto one of the posts, that will give you more height to take off."

"Well done, Sol! That will be perfect. The posts are even taller than the tree stump I took off from when I flew to the top of Blackrock. I'll need to take my cape off before we go, or I won't be able to flap my wings properly. Right, let's do this!"

The friends started to rush towards the wooden fence – which was actually a beach groyne. Adrenaline surged through their veins – they were going home. Nothing could stop them now!

And then Aubrey felt himself being grabbed

from behind by a force the like of which he had never felt before. Both his hat and Sol fell off, and the salamander scurried away to save himself. In an instant Aubrey was upside down, being held by his legs. And then he was being carried quickly away, his vision partly obscured by his cape, which had wrapped itself around his head.

He called out in desperation to whatever creature had hold of him. "Get off me. Get off me! Let me go. I want to go home."

And then he heard the muffled voice of the people-creature called Mick.

"Stop gobbling, you stupid bird. You're going to be in big trouble when I get you back to the barn. Making me come all the way down here to catch you. Mark my words, you feathered pest, I wouldn't be surprised if there was turkey fricassee on the menu tonight."

Aubrey was carried back to the Five Wards Turkey Farm to meet his fate. As he was taken off the beach, still upside down, Aubrey briefly caught sight of what appeared to be a female people-creature. She was running down the beach towards the people-creature called Mick, waving her arms. But then she stumbled and fell, hitting her head on the groyne.

Aubrey didn't see her again. Meanwhile, the Island of Animaux began to fade away, moving to its next, as yet unknown, destination on planet Earth.

And at the same time, the grandfather clock in Aubrey's front room, for the first time since it was made many years before, stopped.

No more *tick*. No more *tock*.

TWO
STRANGE DAYS

Island of Animaux location:
- » latitude 27° south
- » longitude 109° west

It was a gloriously sunny Saturday morning and Clifford was enjoying what he thought was a well-deserved lie-in. He lay back in bed, his front flippers behind his head, relaxing and gazing at the ceiling.

It had been three weeks since Aubrey had vanished.

Clifford and Walli had looked all over the house and in the garden on the night he had disappeared, but there was no sign of him. They had spoken to nearly all the creatures in Wincot, but no one had seen the turkey. They had phoned Audrey, his sister, but she hadn't heard from him. And neither had his parents, who were both long-term residents in the Wincot Senior Citizens' Home.

Finally, Clifford and Walli had reported Aubrey missing to the Crow police. The police had conducted their enquiries with their usual efficiency. This had included strutting around with magnifying glasses held in their wings, looking at nothing in particular, carrying out frequent dawn raids at Hughie Curlew's sweet shop, always managing to 'accidentally' peck large amounts of the confectionery as they looked for 'evidence', and congregating in the yew tree in Aubrey's front garden for long, noisy and apparently pointless cawing sessions.

Their exhaustive investigation at an end, the Crow police had to admit defeat. They closed their file on the missing Aubrey, suggesting that one of two things had happened to him. Either he had somehow evaporated or imploded in the Cabinet of Esvaniss, with his atoms and molecules either wafting away or being accidentally breathed in by Clifford and Walli. Or he had never existed at all and was just a figment of all other creatures' imaginations. The Crow police believed that the second possibility was the more likely, despite all the witness statements and other evidence to the contrary, including photographs of Aubrey.

And so Aubrey was gone, and Clifford and Walli had his house to themselves.

"Strange days," thought Clifford as he nestled down in the bed, quackling with pleasure at his snug-as-a-bug-in-a-rug feeling. He turned and looked at the alarm clock on the bedside table. It was showing 12.10pm, and he was suddenly worried.

"Walli, Walli," he called out at the top of his voice. "Where's my breakfast?" Clifford waited impatiently for a few seconds, then his irritation subsided when he heard Walli coming up the stairs. She appeared at the door to the bedroom.

"What took you so long?" he said very rudely. "And just look at the time! I was expecting my breakfast to be served at 10.30am. It's nearly lunchtime now."

Walli took a deep breath and counted to ten. Clifford had been increasingly snappy with her, for no apparent reason, for the past few weeks, and she was getting a little tired of his attitude. This was definitely not how you were supposed to treat a friend. But after finishing counting to ten, and since she was a very good-natured warthog, she maintained her cool.

"I was cleaning the kitchen. Already this morning I've been to Maureen Moose's Mini Mart and done the weekly shopping. And I've cleaned the rest of the house, except for this room. That included cleaning the bathroom, although you had left the toilet in a disgusting state. Could you please flush it after you've used it?"

"Don't be so sensitive," Clifford replied

dismissively. "You've seen it all before. Anyway, it goes with the job."

"And what job is that, Clifford?" asked Walli, beginning to simmer with rage.

"Keeping the house clean and tidy, of course. Someone's got to do it, and because you're a girl you've got to agree that it's your natural role."

"Natural role?! How is doing the cleaning my natural role?"

"I'm surprised you need to ask me that question," replied Clifford, sitting up in bed. "Throughout the ages it's been the job of males to be brave and clever and earn all the money. And it's been the job of females to clean and cook and look nice and not disturb the males when they are doing important things."

Walli carefully loaded her verbal artillery. She was just about to give Clifford both barrels when he held up his right front flipper to stop her.

"Don't interrupt when I am talking. It's very rude. I've noticed that your manners are not as good as they used to be. Now, for my breakfast I'd like a big plate of hot buttered crumpets, washed down with a cup of warm, milky tea with five spoons of sugar in it. But before you prepare my order, could you pass me my green cardigan? It's on the chair over there. I want to wear it in bed. And could you put my bunny rabbit slippers beside the bed, so I can step straight into them when I get up after having breakfast? I'll let you know when I want you to run my bath for me."

Walli glared at the platypus, barely able to control herself as a hot magma of outrage welled up inside her. And then she erupted with terrifying force. "HOW DARE YOU, CLIFFORD? HOW DARE YOU?"

The explosion took Clifford by surprise, and he bobbed and weaved as best he could to avoid the full force of Walli's blast. The platypus then tried to defuse the situation, although his choice of words was clumsy. "Calm down, Walli. If you're not careful, you'll blow a fuse."

The words were like a red rag to her. "Don't tell me to calm down, you naughty, naughty platypus! Ever since Aubrey disappeared, you've changed, Clifford. Changed completely. You've become lazy, greedy, selfish, rude and disrespectful."

Clifford was surprised at the length of his crime sheet, and attempted to defend himself. But Walli was having none of it.

"Don't interrupt me. You did that earlier, but I'm

too cross to let it happen again. Yes – you're lazy. You quit both your jobs at the leisure centre the day after Aubrey vanished. Since then, you've done nothing but lounge about the house all day, getting up late, making a terrible mess and expecting me to run around after you. That includes doing the cleaning and making all your food. And the only money we've got coming in is what *I* earn from my jobs at Rina's and the Senior Citizens' Home. Why should I have to do two jobs and then look after you when I get home? And *I* had to ask all the creatures if they'd seen Aubrey and call the Crow police. You didn't lift a flipper to help. Instead you sat in Aubrey's armchair in the front room watching the TV."

Walli ploughed on, leaving Clifford with nowhere to hide. "Yes – you're greedy. You've started to eat far too much. You used to be very fit when you were a lifeguard and a football coach. But look at you now, with your jelly belly! You take no exercise and you've put on a lot of weight. You're so out of condition that you puff and pant even when doing simple things, like walking up the stairs.

"And you're selfish. You keep fixing yourself midnight feasts when you can't possibly be hungry after everything you've eaten during the day. And I've lost count of the number of times you've drunk all the milk and eaten all the bread during your feasts, leaving me nothing for my cereal in the morning or to make sandwiches for my lunch. So I have to work on an empty tummy – and then you expect me to make you a big meal when I get home!

"And you're rude. The way you spoke to me this morning is just another example. I am not your slave! If you want something to eat, then get up and make it yourself. And tidy up afterwards! And be considerate of others when you use the bathroom.

"And you're disrespectful. Where did you get the idea that females are better suited to certain types of work? Where is that written? Why shouldn't females have the same chances as males? What gives males the right to have all the fun while females are expected to live their lives in the shadows, making things 'nice' for the males? Wake up and smell the coffee, Clifford! Your views are prehistoric and will get you into big trouble if you persist in believing them and sharing them with others.

"And, talking of being disrespectful, the way you have behaved to Aubrey since he vanished is just ghastly. Here you are, in *his* bed instead of your one in the back bedroom. And you moved in the day after he vanished! You've started to wear his cardigan and his slippers. And you're even behaving like him! No, let me correct that – you're behaving even worse than he did! Aubrey was never disrespectful like you are." Walli had nearly run out of words. But she had saved an important, select few for her concluding remarks.

"I'm very cross with you, Clifford. And disappointed. You are no longer the nice, funny Clifford that I once knew. You have become an obnoxious monster. What on Animaux has happened to you?"

Clifford sat staring at Walli, his bill wide open. He was dumbstruck. He had never received such a big telling-off before, not even when he was younger and had played with a box of matches, carelessly discarded by a people-creature, and had accidentally set fire to his home. Of course, his mother had been very cross with him, but she had been more concerned that he was OK and that they were safe.

He looked at Walli, and tears suddenly appeared in his eyes. "Walli, my dear friend," he gasped in a weak, tremulous voice. "I'm so sorry for the way I have behaved, being useless and awful when you needed me to be strong. But I haven't known what to do."

The warthog looked at Clifford, concern etched on her face. "What do you mean, Clifford? I don't understand."

Tears started to roll down Clifford's cheeks. He was clearly in great distress. Walli climbed on the bed and gave him a big hug to comfort him. The platypus sobbed for a while, his tears splashing on the bedclothes and on Walli's shoulder.

At last he calmed down. After wiping his streaming bill on the back of his left front flipper, Clifford felt able to answer Walli's question. "I'm sorry I've been so horrible to you, Walli. I really am. I didn't mean any of it. It's just that I can't accept that Aubrey isn't here any more. And I can't cope with how lost I feel. He was here one minute and then he vanished. Where has he gone? Why couldn't we find him? What should we have done differently? I've been so sad these past three weeks. I should have told you how I felt, but I was scared to."

"Why were you scared, Clifford?" asked Walli, feeling distressed that she hadn't realised how bad her friend had been feeling.

"Because I'm supposed to be a big, brave platypus. I'm supposed to have a solution for every problem. But I'm not brave and I don't have an answer. And then I looked at you. You've been so organised, speaking to everyone and rushing everywhere and trying so hard to find Aubrey. And working so hard at your jobs and doing all the shopping and making all my food. While I just feel totally useless at not being able to help."

Walli looked at her dear friend and gave him an

extra-big hug. She placed both her front trotters on his shoulders and looked into his eyes. "Clifford, you're right – I have been very busy. But I should never have been so busy that I couldn't see how unhappy you were."

Little smiles broke out on both their faces.

"Let me tell you a story, Clifford. It might help. Quite a long time ago, when I was still in South Africa, something terrible happened. It was the worst thing I had ever experienced. My Uncle Narciso, who was my mum's elder brother and who was a huge, clever and much-loved warthog, had stopped by a watering hole one day, on his way back home after a great time rolling in the dust. As he was drinking, a lion sneaked up and jumped on him. There was a terrible fight, and Uncle Narciso fought as hard as he could. But eventually the lion was too strong … and poor Uncle Narciso was no more."

Walli paused. She could see her uncle clearly in her mind – how he had let her ride on his back when she was little, how he pulled funny faces at her that made her laugh so much, how he warned her about how dangerous lions were and that you should never take your eyes off them. It was painful for her to talk about his passing but she carried on, knowing that doing so would help Clifford.

"Of course, my aunt was devastated. We all were. We mourned for days. But then Grandma Venus gathered us together one evening and told us about the five stages of grief. The first stage is *denial*, when you don't believe what has happened. The next stage is *anger*, when you might wish that the bad thing had happened to someone else. Next comes *bargaining*, when you ask yourself if you could have done anything that would have stopped the nasty thing happening. Then comes *depression*, where you feel very sad. And finally comes *acceptance*, where you acknowledge what has happened and come to terms with it. But you never forget the creature that has passed away, or stop loving them. And you will always wish they were still here."

Clifford had listened very carefully to Walli's story.

She continued, "My dear friend, I think part of you is still in the denial stage. And you are denying things so strongly that you've actually started to turn into Aubrey. But don't worry – I'll give you all the help and support you need and we'll get through this together. And I want you to know that, every night since Aubrey disappeared, I've cried for him. Sometimes I've gone downstairs and sat in the Cabinet of Esvaniss. It was the last place we saw him, and it seems to bring me closer to poor Aubrey. I miss him terribly. I hope he is well and happy, wherever he is."

Clifford looked fondly at Walli, then gave her an enormous hug. "Thank you, Walli. What you just said means a tremendous amount to me. From now on, I will be the Clifford Platypus you know, not the nasty, self-absorbed creature you've had to put up with over the past few weeks. We will never stop looking for our friend. Never! And I will take better care of myself. I will eat less and exercise much more. I will do my fair share around the house and see if I can get my old jobs back. And I will try to accept what has happened to Aubrey."

SCENE TWO – THE VICIOUS VISITOR

The platypus kept his word. He once again became a good friend to Walli, doing his fair share of work both inside and outside the house. He also put himself on a diet and embarked on the greatest fitness regime the Island of Animaux had ever seen. When we wasn't jogging, he was swimming. When he wasn't swimming, he was shadow-boxing. And when he wasn't shadow-boxing, he was skipping. In no time the sleek, fit Clifford had returned. As had one of his old jobs. Once again Clifford was the lifeguard at Wincot Leisure Centre, replacing Anusha Alpaca, whose long, hairy coat quickly became waterlogged whenever she entered the water, meaning that the creatures swimming in the pool often had to save *her* rather than the other way around.

Time flew by for Clifford and Walli. As they sat one late afternoon at the kitchen table in Aubrey's house, two weeks after the 'stages of grief' discussion, they only had one thing to talk about: their missing friend. There had still been no sign of him, and they had begun to accept that he would never be coming back. But rather than be sad, they amused each other by telling stories about him, about funny things he had said and done. About how, when Aubrey tried really hard, things always went wrong. And about how things always seemed to turn out right in the end. He had been such a good, true friend to them. He had welcomed them into his life and had shared his house with them when they had arrived – by accident – on Animaux with nowhere to stay. They would always love him.

Their fond reminiscing was suddenly interrupted by someone hammering on the front door.

"Is it him?" asked Walli, her heart fluttering as she looked at Clifford with wide eyes. "Do you think Aubrey is back?"

Clifford didn't reply. Instead, they jumped off their chairs and ran to the front door as fast as their trotters and flippers could carry them.

Flinging open the door with the intention of leaping on Aubrey and showering him with hugs and kisses, they found themselves facing not a turkey, but a rat.

"Good evening, Master Ploppypus and Miss Piglet," began Rick, oozing his usual acidic brand of 'charm'. "I thought I'd stop by to see if it was true."

"Oh, it's you, Rick," replied Clifford, massively disappointed not to be talking to his feathered friend. "Is what true?"

Rick gave a greasy, self-satisfied smirk. He could hardly contain his joy as he answered. "That Aubrey has snuffed it. That he's kicked the bucket. That he's

turned up his toes. That he's brown bread. That he's dead!" Clearly satisfied with his choice of words, Rick did a celebratory paw pump.

"What happened to his mangy body? Did you put it in an old cardboard box and bury it in the Bone Zone? Or did you chuck it in the dustbin with the rest of the rubbish?"

The platypus and the warthog were seething. But they weren't prepared to play the rat at his own game. He was clearly trying to antagonise them, but they vowed to stay strong and not sink to his slimy, subterranean level.

"He hasn't died," said Walli, truly hoping this wasn't actually the case. "He's just disappeared. But I'm sure he'll be back soon."

"And he's been gone for the past five weeks," added Clifford. "Looks like you're out of touch, Rick, if you've only just heard the news. But since you don't have any friends, I'm not surprised that you always find out about things way after everybody else."

"I did hear about it weeks ago," replied the rat, dented by the 'no friends' remark, which was painfully close to the truth. "But I've been savouring the moment. And it has been sweet to taste. That bird deserved everything he got. Mr 'High and Mighty' Aubrey the Turkey. Always thinking he was better than everyone else. Always taking advantage of poor, defenceless, good-natured creatures—"

"What are you talking about, Rick?" interjected Clifford, growing tired of the rat's nonsense talk.

"I'm talking about me – poor old Rick Rat!" shot back the rodent, cross at being interrupted. "Aubrey had it coming. Ever since he forced me to drink his stinging nettle fizz. Ever since he told Georgina to choose Reuben Ram as her boyfriend instead of me. Ever since he asked Geraldine to sting my tail with one of her tentacles. Well, I'm *happy* that he's snuffed it. I'm *happy* that I'll never see him again. And I'm *happy* that you two are sad because he's not here any more."

Clifford had had enough. Rick needed to be put in his place. The platypus got straight to the point. "When you snuff it, Rick, no one will mourn for you. Or put flowers on your grave. In fact, there will probably be a party. And I will lead the singing!"

The platypus and the rat squared up to each other, both thinking that right was on their side.

Walli had heard enough. Sensing the possibility of a fight starting, she pushed between them – a tusked referee. She also had some important points to make to them. "That's enough, boys. I don't want to hear any more. This is not a nice conversation, and you should both be ashamed of yourselves."

Her unexpected intervention had the desired effect, and the two creatures calmed down. Satisfied, Walli turned to her friend.

"Clifford, I think you should say sorry to Rick. That wasn't a very nice thing you just said to him. I am sure there are many creatures who care about him and will be very sad when he finally goes paws up. Although that probably won't be for a long time."

Clifford was reluctant to apologise to the rat. He had regretted his comments to Rick the moment they had left his bill, but felt that since he hadn't started the argument, it should be the rodent who apologised first. But after a small amount of internal grumbling he decided to offer an olive branch.

"Sorry, Rick. That wasn't very nice of me. I take it back. I wish you a long and healthy life, and I'm sure you'll be missed when you are gone."

Walli gave Clifford a little smile and nodded to show her contentment with his words. Then she faced Rick. "Your turn, Rick. Please say sorry to Clifford – and me, for that matter – for all the nasty things you just said about poor Aubrey."

Rick looked at both of them and bowed his head slightly. Clearly, he was selecting his words with great care, and Walli and Clifford looked forward to his gushing contrition.

Then Rick looked up, a nasty smirk playing on his lips. But instead of saying anything, he blew the most enormous raspberry in their direction, spraying them with his stinking spittle.

"Me apologise to you!" he squeaked. "Not a rat's chance! I meant every word, and I hope the stupid turkey – if he's still alive, which I doubt – is miserable every day that his rotten carcass still has a heart beating within it."

Thoroughly delighted, Rick chuckled loudly then turned tail and scuttled back down the garden path, his mission complete.

Clifford was tempted to go after him and to extract, with force if necessary, an apology. But Walli whispered, "No, Clifford", and instead they watched Rick go through the garden gate, then begin the journey back to his pipe home.

The two friends stepped back into the house, closing the front door behind them. Clifford looked across the front room to the far wall. The Cabinet of Esvaniss was still there, unmoved since Aubrey had vanished from it. The platypus turned to Walli.

"You said that you've sometimes sat in the cabinet and that it brings you closer to Aubrey. Do you mind if we both sit in it now for a few minutes? I would like to feel him with us again. It would be nice."

Walli nuzzled against him. "Of course, Clifford. Yes, it would be very nice."

They began to walk towards the cabinet, but they were stopped by more hammering on the front door.

"If it's Rick again, I'm going to stick his tail where the sun don't shine!" shouted Clifford. Before Walli could stop him he had spun around, rushed over to the door and flung it open so hard that it crashed against the wall.

"You've asked for it!" he shouted, anger filling his body. "Stand by to receive a flipper piledriver!"

Scene Three – Bottled Hope

But then Clifford stopped in his tracks. For standing on the doorstep, looking at him with great bemusement, was Claude Crane Fly.

After flying thousands of circuits around the Singsong Bay lighthouse, Claude's muscles were bigger than ever. And he was glistening with sweat, presumably thanks to his twenty-kilometre flight to Aubrey's house.

Remembering the trick he had played on Claude the last time they met – he had fooled the crane fly into chasing him to the lighthouse so that Claude would be entranced by the light – Clifford decided to proceed with great caution.

"Sorry, Claude, but I thought you were someone else. No offence intended. We don't want any trouble. Aubrey isn't here any more. And what happened to poor Claudette really was an accident, I promise you."

Walli pushed past him to say her piece to the crane fly.

"Claude, I wanted to give you my deepest apology. I didn't mean to eat Claudette, really I didn't. It's just that I hadn't had any food for such a long time, as I'd been stuck in a long, dark tunnel. I was so hungry when I got out, I wasn't thinking clearly. Please say you forgive me."

Claude looked at them. He was still bemused, but he had come on a mission, and decided that now was the time to share it with the platypus and the warthog.

"My long nights of flying around the lighthouse gave me plenty of time to think about what happened to my little sister. I have felt a range of emotions over the past few months, from denial to anger to depression. But now I have accepted what has happened. There is nothing I can do to change the past. Claudette was such a sweet young thing – she didn't deserve what happened to her. But I do know that she was happy when she passed away. She had a new boyfriend, Aubrey, and she had so much to look forward to. So I don't bear either of you any grudges – or the turkey, for that matter. You said that he's gone away?"

Relieved that Claude had forgiven them, Clifford felt able to answer the question without fear of having to duck or defensively cover his face with his flippers. "He disappeared about five weeks ago. He was doing a magic trick, something went wrong, and we haven't seen him since."

Claude listened carefully, understanding the seriousness of the situation. "Well, I'm sorry for him. And for you, as his friends. I hope he is OK and comes home soon. Oh, yeah – I need to tell you why I've come. As you know, I fly around the lighthouse all night, stopping only when the sun starts to rise. Well, one morning, quite a few weeks ago, I noticed something glinting on the beach at Singsong Bay. The sun's rays must have caught it. I had meant to take a look, see what it was, but I was too tired after my flying. Anyway, this morning I buzzed over to it. It's addressed to you, so here it is." Claude handed Clifford a square bottle made of green glass that he had been holding with one of his many legs.

"And how long ago did you say you first saw it?" enquired Clifford.

"Oh, about five weeks. Give or take a day." His duty completed, Claude had other things to attend to. "I need to buzz off. I should be able to get back to the lighthouse in time for a nap. Then I have another busy night ahead. My record is four thousand circuits of the lighthouse in a night, and I'm going to try and beat that tonight. See you again sometime."

Giving Walli and Clifford a wave with three of his legs, including the one that had been holding the bottle, Claude started to rotate his wings and immediately soared into the air. The two friends watched him as he altered direction and headed south-west, on course for Singsong Bay.

Walli and Clifford closed the front door.

"What is it, Clifford?" asked Walli, gesturing to the bottle he was holding.

"I'm not sure. Let's go in the kitchen and take a look. The light is better in there."

The two went into the kitchen and sat at the table. Clifford examined the bottle. "It's Galliform Bumblefoot Medicine," he said, reading the label. "Whatever is that? Hang on, there's something inside the bottle. It looks like a piece of paper."

Clifford turned the bottle over and peered through the glass. And then he read out loud, his voice trembling, the words written on the paper.

"Dear finder, please deliver this message to Clifford Platypus and Walli Hog. They live in the little house at the end of Fluffy Cloud Lane. Thank you."

The platypus gulped. Straight away, with shaking flippers, he uncorked the bottle and tipped out the message within. He smoothed it open and eagerly read the words written on the paper, then read them again – and again.

"What is it, Clifford?" asked Walli, very concerned. Her friend looked frantic.

"It's from Aubrey!" Clifford gasped. "He needs our help! At least, he needed it five weeks ago! That's how long the bottle has been on the beach. Oh no, Walli, I think we're too late!"

THREE

HOMEWARD BOUND

Island of Animaux location:

» latitude 40° south

» longitude 174° east

S C E N E O N E – O P E R A T I O N F I N D T H A T T U R K E Y !

My dear friends,

I doubt that you will ever read this message, but I needed to write it anyway.

As you must know, something went wrong with the disappearing spell. I think I have travelled to the world that you both come from and that you have told me so much about. I am in a place called the Silly Islands, near somewhere called Grate Britten. I am well and I'm living in a building on a farm with lots of other turkeys. Unfortunately, they only speak Turkese, so I can't understand them.

There are also some people-creatures here. I can understand them but they can't understand me. I'm not sure I like them, as one has been a bit rough and hurt me.

I think I told you about the Great Salamander? He used to own the Cabinet of Esvaniss and he is here with me – we both disappeared to the same place! His name is Sol and he's very nice. In a few minutes we are going down to the sea and when we get there we will try to return to Animaux, although I'm not sure how.

Sol told me that he got the disappearing spell from the Weird Sisters and accidentally sprinkled it on himself rather than the cabinet. And I must have trodden on some of the spell. That's how I was able to disappear. Also, the words to the spell were wrong. That's why Sol and I both came here without the cabinet. Could you visit the Weird Sisters and get some more of the spell? Then perhaps Sol and I can come back.

I've never told you how much I love you both. I wish that I had. You have been so kind to me, and I will never forget you.

Goodbye.

Aubrey xx

Sitting at the kitchen table in Aubrey's house, Clifford almost managed to stay composed as he read the message out loud. But as he got to the last few sentences his voice began to tremble. The platypus was deeply moved by what Aubrey had written.

It was Saturday evening, about an hour and a half since Clifford had uncorked the green medicine bottle in which Aubrey had stored his message. Clifford had read the message to Walli three times. They had quickly decided on their next steps. Clifford had phoned Douglas Duck and asked him to come straight to the house. As Georgina didn't have a phone in her shed, Clifford asked Douglas to pop around and tell her to come as well. And just over an hour later the two arrived, after their steep, exhausting walk up Fluffy Cloud Lane. Douglas had spent the entire journey crouching, jockey-like, on the wheezing, sweating Georgina's back.

Georgina and Douglas, sitting at the kitchen table with Clifford and Walli, stared at the platypus as he put Aubrey's note down. The goat and the duck absorbed its content in silence, not sure what to say or do next.

Clifford thought he had better kick things off. "The message makes it clear that Aubs is still alive. At least, he was alive five weeks ago, which is when he disappeared and about the time Claude Crane Fly spotted the bottle on the shore at Singsong Bay. Aubs said that he was going down to the sea with Sol, to try and find a way back to Animaux. That's where he must have thrown the bottle into the sea, although how it ended up on Animaux is anyone's guess. Clearly they weren't successful in their attempt because if they had been, then we would have heard from Aubs by now. Does my thinking make sense?"

Georgina and Douglas nodded, still silent. Walli also nodded. Clifford continued. "Very good. Now there are some parts of Aubs' note that make sense to Walli and me, but there are other parts we don't understand."

"Strangely enough, I had exactly the same thought," said Georgina, breaking her silence. "Maybe there are parts that confuse you that I understand and vice versa? Shall we compare notes?"

Clifford enthusiastically clapped his front flippers together. They were making progress. "Great idea, Georgie. Right, Aubs says that he's on the Silly Islands, near Grate Britten. Walli and I remember, from our geography lessons at school, a place called the Scilly Isles. And it's actually spelt Great Britain. So we think that's where Aubs is. And then something he wrote got us really worried."

"What's that?" asked Georgina. "Didn't he say he was living with other turkeys? That seems OK. Although the people-creatures don't sound very nice."

Walli continued. "He said he was on a farm. So we think it's a turkey farm. And that is not at all good, based on our knowledge of what turkey farms are for."

Georgina and Douglas gave her a quizzical look.

Douglas's curiosity got the better of him. "So, what are they for?"

Clifford took over. "Something happens in the world we come from that doesn't happen here. There's no easy way to say it. Creatures eat other creatures."

"What do you mean, creatures eat other creatures? What nonsense!" quacked Douglas loudly and dismissively. "If that's your idea of a joke, I don't think it's very funny."

"We're telling the truth, Douglas," said Walli. "Remember what I told you about how I came here – that a lion was trying to eat me and I escaped by running into a hole? Creatures eating other creatures is normal in the world beyond this island."

Clifford realised he had to explain things more clearly to the flustered duck. "Turkey farms are where people-creatures – or humans, as Walli and I call them – keep turkeys to fatten them up. And when the turkeys are nice and plump, the humans take them away and turn them into roast dinners. In short, they kill them and eat them."

"But that is monstrous!" shouted Douglas, clearly outraged. He was spoiling for a fight with one of these humans, even though he had no idea what such a creature was.

"Perhaps it is monstrous. But it's the way things are, and there's nothing we can do to change the situation. The only hope for Aubs is that the other turkeys are not plump enough yet to be taken to be 'converted'."

"Converted?" asked Georgina.

"Yes – converted into sausages or drumsticks or turkey twizzlers."

"But what if we're too late?"

"Let's not think about that," said Walli. "It is too terrible."

The friends were all silent for a few seconds.

"Let's get back to the message, to see if we can

make sense of the rest of it," said Walli, trying to dispel the cloud of depression that had descended on them. "Georgina and Douglas. Do you know who or what the Weird Sisters are?"

"I've heard of them," said Georgina. "Harry Hyena tried to chat me up once. I told him I wasn't interested, but he was determined. Harry tried his hardest to impress me but his stories were boring, his jokes weren't funny, and because he had a cold his nose kept running and he kept licking the snot with his tongue. It was disgusting." Georgina stopped and shuddered as her mind flashed back to Harry and his tongue. But then she remembered what question she was answering. "Anyway, for some reason Harry told me about the Sisters. Apparently, they are three magical black cats who live in a cave on the other side of Mount Verticus. They can cast spells to order, although they charge a high price for doing so. And they will only do business with creatures that have a black heart – whatever that is. Harry explained how to get to their cave. I can show you the way first thing in the morning if you like. It's getting dark, so it's too dangerous to go now."

Georgina was correct. Through the kitchen

window, the friends could see the sun beginning to set.

Clifford decided to end the discussion with a call to action. "Georgie, we all agree. Let's go in the morning. We need a good night's rest, as tomorrow will be a big day. The day that we rescue Aubs and Sol and bring them back to Animaux!"

The friends slept well that night, with Clifford remaining in Aubrey's bed, Georgina joining Walli in the back bedroom, and Douglas sleeping in the bath, with some blankets and pillows that Walli had given him.

The following morning was again wonderfully warm and sunny and they all rose early, had a nice breakfast then started to get ready for the journey up Mount Verticus and down the other side to meet the Weird Sisters.

While Georgina was outside, sharpening her horns against the yew tree, and Douglas was upstairs in the toilet, Walli had a quick discussion with Clifford.

"Clifford, didn't Georgina say the Weird Sisters were cats?"

Clifford nodded. "Yes, three black cats, I think she said."

Walli was worried. "But aren't cats the same as lions, only smaller?"

The platypus could see where she was heading. "Well, they are from the same family of animals, but they're not nearly as fierce. In fact, when I was in Australia I used to know a very friendly ginger tomcat called Tom. He wasn't fierce at all – actually, he had lost most of his teeth because he was so old and so he could only give gummy bites."

Walli wasn't convinced. To her, any lion-like creature should be treated with great caution and suspicion. "Even so, I'm not very keen on meeting the cats. Just in case they want to eat me, you understand?"

Clifford slipped into big brother mode. "Yes, I understand. Don't worry. I'll protect you, Walli. And I'll make sure I take a few secret weapons with me, just in case!" With that he headed up the stairs, passing Douglas, who was scurrying in the opposite direction, worried that the platypus was about to discover the terrible smell he had left in the bathroom.

Walli put her hat on and walked out of the house and over to Georgina and Douglas. "We'd better be off. The return journey to the Weird Sisters will take quite a while."

"Well, I'm ready," said Georgina. "And I'm sure Clifford won't be long. Are you ready, Douglas?"

Douglas had been quieter than usual that morning. Normally, he had something to say about everything, so it was clear that something was on his mind. He mumbled an answer to Walli's question. "I won't be coming to visit the Weird Sisters."

This caught Walli and Georgina completely by surprise. Georgina tried to get more information from him. "Why not, Douglas? It's better that we all go – there's safety in numbers. And this is all about saving Aubrey. Don't you want to help?"

Douglas was a duck who preferred to avoid taking risks whenever possible. That was the main reason he had never had a girlfriend, and why he was unadventurous with his choice of food. "Of course I want to help. I'd be delighted to see Aubrey come home. But perhaps the best way for me to help is to stay here while you visit the Sisters, in case Aubrey comes back in the meantime. If he does, then I'll make him a cup of tea. And if he doesn't, then I'll let you know when you return. Yes. I will guard Aubrey's house!"

Douglas was clearly very happy with his plan, and gave himself a self-congratulatory quack of approval. He then waddled into the house, over to Aubrey's armchair and sat on it, adjusting his fat little bottom until he was comfortable. And then he tucked his head under his wing and fell asleep.

Walli and Georgina stared at each other in silent amazement. So it would just be the three of them going to see the Sisters. But perhaps this would be best, as Douglas's little legs would have struggled to keep up with them. And speed might be important when you were visiting magical cats…

Then Georgina remembered what Harry had told her. "Walli, we will need to pay the Sisters for the spell. I have got two gold eagles. Do you have any money?"

"Yes, I've got five eagles. I've put them in the inner lining of my hat to keep them safe on the journey. Would you like me to put yours there as well?"

"Yes, please," said Georgina. To Walli's great surprise, the goat spat the eagles out onto the ground. They had been lodged in her cheeks. "I really must buy myself a purse," she said before wiping some dribble from her lips.

Carefully Walli picked up the dripping, slippery coins and put them inside her hat, making sure they weren't too close to the dry ones.

Then Clifford came bounding down the stairs, a duffel bag over his shoulder. "One minute," he said before rushing into the kitchen, quickly finding whatever he was looking for and then coming straight back.

"Before we go, there's an important thing we need to arrange for later. In Aubs' message he said that there were humans at the farm and they were rough. We need to prepare for this. We need to take backup, to give us an advantage."

"Who will be our backup?" asked Walli.

"You'll find out," Clifford said with a smile. Then he leant over and whispered something in Georgina's ear. She grinned and then clip-clopped over to Douglas. She woke him and whispered in his ear. He also smiled and nodded, obviously understanding what she had said.

The whispering over, Clifford clapped his front flippers together. "Right, let's go – there's no time to lose," he said. Walli, Georgina and the platypus went out of the front door to start their journey

"Why didn't Douglas want to come?" Clifford asked as the three friends left the front garden and started to climb the mountainside.

"He said he'd guard the house in case Aubrey came back," said Georgina. "And in case he didn't come back."

Clifford laughed. "Sometimes Douglas is a little odd. I've never understood why he only eats bananas. That seems a very boring diet. He invited me for tea at his place once – you know, his apartment over his curtain shop. All he offered me were mashed banana sandwiches and banana juice to drink. And the sandwich bread was stale. I think he got it from the dustbin at the back of Maureen Moose's Mini Mart, where she throws away all her out-of-date stock. He doesn't like spending money if he can help it. And do you remember his barbecue on the day of Aubs' surprise party? All he had to offer were whole unripe green bananas! Whoever heard of a barbecued banana?! It was lucky that Martha the Manatee was there and had brought potato salad and coleslaw and vegetables and other delicious things."

"It was a lovely feast," said Walli. She fondly remembered the gorgeous spicy, grilled mushrooms.

SCENE TWO – SPELLS AND SPILLS

For the rest of their journey, the friends discussed many things. But their discussion always came back to Aubrey, and how they were all prepared to do whatever it took to get him home safely.

They reached the blasted oak tree at the far end of Mount Verticus more quickly than they had expected. Without pausing, they started down the rocky path that led to the Weird Sisters' cave. Walli had to be helped by Georgina and Clifford on more than one occasion as she found the path very slippery. Once she skidded, and would have gone over the edge if Clifford and Georgina hadn't grabbed her.

The cave entrance was dark and forbidding. The torch fixed in the rock above it, a flaming beacon at night, had gone out and looked like a twisted, scorched bone.

Clifford was leading the trio. He hesitated for a second before entering the cave, suddenly a little fearful of what they might encounter. But then he remembered that Aubrey was depending on them and he pressed on, with Walli and Georgina following very close behind.

Unlike the one outside, the torches in the cave were still burning. The friends moved cautiously, making sure they didn't bump into any rocky outcrops or skid on the slick stone floor.

They entered the central chamber, as Rick Rat had done many months before. The fire under the cauldron had gone out and the contents of the pot, if it had any, were still and quiet.

The Weird Sisters must have been busy recently, judging by the enormous piles of gold and silver coins on the floor. Next to them, a pile of precious stones, including diamonds, rubies, emeralds and sapphires, sparkled in the torchlight.

Another pile, the highest of all, consisted of hundreds of tins of sardines. The Sisters would not be going hungry in the months ahead.

And there was a final, grisly pile. It seemed to be made up of parts of creatures – perhaps they had been given in part-payment for spells? It included manes, fur, antlers, tusks, hoof clippings, what looked like a rat's whiskers, three yellowish-orange spots and, most disturbingly, what looked like an ear, perhaps from a cow.

They could hear the faint sound of the sea crashing against the rocks far below the cave entrance. But otherwise there was complete silence in the chamber.

Then the three heard another faint sound.

Snoring.

Still huddling together, Clifford, Walli and Georgina searched for the source of the snoring. They soon found it. Lying in three wicker baskets by the cave wall – no longer wearing their hooded robes, which were thrown on the floor beside each basket – were three black cats, fast asleep. They were all lying comfortably and snoring in complete harmony.

Georgina nervously cleared her throat and whispered to the others. "Do you think we should come back later? They look like they're having a lovely sleep, and they might get cross if we wake them."

Clifford and Walli turned to face her. "We don't have the time, Georgie. They need to help us now."

The three friends turned back to the baskets – only to find that the cats and their robes had vanished. Shocked, they all took a step backwards, their knees knocking.

Immediately they spotted three hooded figures standing in a row on the other side of the chamber. The cats had moved like lightning to dress and reach their current position.

"All hail, you creatures three. Hail to thee, animals with your cloven hooves," the hooded figures said, their voices perfectly synchronised. The figures then turned to look at each other.

"One has flippers," said the figure on the left.

"And the other has got trotters. They're not really cloven hooves, are they?" said the one on the right.

"I'm not sure," said the one on the left.

"Aren't we supposed to know everything?" asked the one on the right.

"I was never good at anatomy," said the one on the left.

"Do you think they noticed us make the mistake?" queried the one on the right.

The one on the left shook her head. "I don't know. I hope not."

"All right, all right, that's enough!" shouted the figure in the middle, clearly exasperated. "Let's focus! We'll go from the top again. Ready?"

The figures faced the three friends again. "All hail, you creatures three. Hail to thee, animals with your cloven hooves *and* flippers *and* trotters."

The figures gave a joint purr of satisfaction and continued. "We know why you are here. We can read your minds. You want more of the disappearing spell we gave to that fake magician, Solomon Salamander. And you want to know the words for the disappearing and reappearing spells. We can give you all this, but it will be expensive. And much more expensive than usual, for we know that none of you has a black heart."

The cats gave another collective purr.

Clifford decided to try to bargain with them. "Weird Sisters, we are three simple creatures who want to rescue our friend, Aubrey the Turkey. We don't have much money. As you've made the spell before and may have a little bit left over, can we get it at a discounted price?"

The Sisters hissed at Clifford, furious with his suggestion. "Silence, Clifford Platypus, prehistoric mammal from the land down under! We can see deep into your heart and mind. We see all your devious plans, and we know your weaknesses. You are not in a position to bargain with us, so save your breath!"

Then the Sisters changed their tone, to something much more friendly. "And please call us the Three Sisters, if you don't mind, Mr Platypus. Weird Sisters makes us sound very strange."

The Three Sisters turned their attention to Walli and resumed their threatening tone. "Hail to thee, Walta Nelson Hogg from South Africa. We see your little heart trembling. You are afraid of us and think we will eat you. We have not tasted warthog before, but perhaps we will later!"

Walli hid behind Clifford and Georgina, her little heart thumping in dread. She cursed herself for coming on this trip.

Then the Sisters turned to Georgina. "Hail to thee, Georgina the Goat. We recommend you add clotted cream to your range of dairy products, as we think there is a good market for it."

The Sisters addressed the friends again. "The spell will cost you seven gold eagles. That's less than we charged the salamander. But the offer is only available today. Walli Hog, please come out from behind your friends. We know you have that much money in your hat. Put it on the pile of gold coins and we will cast the spell."

Walli took the coins from her hat and ran to put them on the correct pile. Then even more quickly, she ran back to her friends, keen to get out of the Sisters' cave as fast as possible.

Satisfied, the Sisters waved their front paws and chanted some strange words. A sparkling, spinning ball about the size of a grapefruit suddenly appeared in front of the Sisters, suspended in mid-air by a mysterious force. One of the Sisters took out an empty paper bag from a pocket in her robe. She opened it under the ball, the Sisters all said, "Done", and the sparkling ball collapsed into glittering powder, which fell into the bag.

The Sister twisted the top of the bag to keep it closed, then tossed it towards the three friends. It landed at Georgina's feet.

Then the Sisters spoke again. "Listen carefully, creatures of the fields and water. You must sprinkle the spell over the *outside* of the cabinet. And these are the words of the spells. You must say them correctly.

"To disappear in the cabinet, you must say:

Mysterious forces
Hear me clear,
Make this cabinet
Disappear.

"And to reappear you must say:

Mysterious forces
Hear me clear,
Make this cabinet
Reappear.

"Got it?"

"Yes, understood," Clifford said. "Thanks for your time. We'll go now and let you return to your baskets for some well-deserved rest." He turned to Walli and Georgina. "Come on, let's get out of here!"

Walli stowed the paper bag under her hat and the friends started to move quickly to the passageway that led out of the chamber and back towards the cave entrance.

"One moment!" shouted the Sisters. "Our business is not yet done. There is a final price that you must pay in order to leave our cave!"

Clifford stopped and faced them. "Final price? But we paid you seven gold eagles, as you asked. You can't ask us for more."

"We can do whatever we want," replied the Sisters menacingly. "You are in our realm now, and you will pay the full price."

Wanting to leave the cave with no further delay, Clifford decided to go along with the Sisters' request. "Very well. What is the final price?"

"The warthog. She must stay with us, to look after us. And perhaps one day to become our dinner."

Walli squealed in terror. Clifford and Georgina

moved in front of her to shield her from the Sisters. But the Sisters were not to be denied.

"You have no choice. She must stay – or none of you will leave here alive!"

It was time for Clifford to unveil the special things he had gathered at the house. He spoke to the Sisters in a brisk, business-like way, hoping they would know what a good deal looked like when it was offered to them. "I've got something in my bag that you would like more than Walli. Take it instead of her."

"What is it?" asked the Sisters, suddenly curious and apparently forgetting that they could see into Clifford's mind if they wanted. "Is it more gold or precious jewels? Or tins of sardines?"

"It's better than all of those," said Clifford, hoping that it was true. He took the bag from his shoulder and dipped into it. Fishing some objects out and throwing them towards the Sisters he said, rather hopefully, "There are three balls to play with – one for each of you. I know how much cats like chasing balls. You can throw them to each other."

The Sisters gave a familiar hiss of disapproval.

Clifford dipped into his bag again. This time he pulled out a small square of paper. "OK. How about a Pale Blue President? You know, the stamp? It is the pride of Aubrey's collection, but I'm sure he won't mind me giving it to you. It's worth an awful lot of money."

This time the Sisters snarled and spat at him.

Clifford realised he needed to try a different approach. He decided to try to unsettle the Sisters. "Right, you want to play rough? Beware, cats, I've got secret weapons in this bag that I am prepared to use. But if you make me use them, you'll regret it!"

The cats looked at him with disdain. "We have no fear of anything! We are the Three Sisters."

His bluff called, Clifford had no choice but to reveal what was left in his bag. "Don't say I didn't warn you." Dipping deep into the bag, he pulled out weapon number one. "Look – see this mirror. Cats hate seeing their reflections in mirrors. Be terrified, all of you!"

The cats edged forward to look at their reflection.

"Hmm, I'm looking good today," said the Sister on the left.

"And I'm looking even better," said the Sister on the right.

"I must get my hair cut," said the Sister in the centre.

Then they all gave Clifford their best withering gazes.

He knew that his next weapon had better be good, or there was trouble ahead. Clifford dipped into the bag and pulled out a bottle of water. "See, Sisters – I have water. Cats hate water! I will throw it at you and you will become damp and bedraggled. Don't make me do it!"

"You are a rather silly platypus," said the Sister in the centre. "Here we are in our cave, with all the spray from the sea blowing in. We have become used to water and have no fear of it."

Georgina spoke in a low voice to Clifford. "What do we do next?"

Clifford found this an easy choice. "Run!" he shouted at the top of his voice. The three friends set off as fast as they could, reaching the passageway to the cave entrance and then racing along it toward the exit.

But the witches were hard on their heels. They began to fire warning shots – brightly coloured bursts of sparkles whizzed past the friends, bouncing off the ceiling and walls of the passageway.

"This is your final warning!" they shouted. "Stop now or we will turn you all to stone!"

The three friend obeyed and stopped. They were only about ten metres from the cave entrance. So near, and yet so far…

Walli was sobbing. She didn't want to stay with the Sisters. But she wanted her friends to get away safely. If that meant she had to remain, then she would accept this, although it would break her heart. But Clifford wasn't done yet. He whispered to both of them, "I've got one weapon left. I've no idea whether it will work, but here goes nothing."

He pulled something from the bag and carefully placed it on the floor. The Sisters didn't notice it at first, instead confidently striding towards the friends, thinking they had them where they wanted them, in their paws. But then, when they were almost standing on it, they saw what Clifford had deployed. Immediately they jumped in the air, yowling in panic, then they turned around and rushed back down the passageway to the safety of their chamber. They wouldn't feel brave enough to come out again for many weeks.

Seizing their chance, full of relief, the friends ran out of the cave and all the way up the cliff path, only stopping to catch their breath when they reached the blasted oak tree at the top.

"What was the last secret weapon?" gasped Georgina. "In all the excitement, I didn't see what you put on the floor."

Clifford laughed. "Believe it or not, just a cucumber. So it *is* true – cats really are afraid of them! Perhaps it reminded them of a snake."

Georgina and Walli also laughed. The friends took the time to enjoy the sunlight and the fresh air, both of which had been absent in the cave of the Weird Sisters.

Their short rest over, it was time to travel back to Aubrey's house. At Georgina's recommendation, Clifford and Walli climbed on her back. The goat started to gallop at a tremendous speed, the platypus and the warthog hanging on for dear life and enjoying every moment, particularly when Georgina jumped over any boulders or fallen tree trunks that stood in their way.

When they arrived back at the house, they found Douglas having a cup of tea with a surprise guest. However, the guest was not Aubrey the Turkey, as they had hoped, but Reuben the Ram. Georgina rushed over and gave him a big hug.

"A-ha – our backup is here!" said Clifford with a smile.

The friends then got ready to disappear in the Cabinet of Esvaniss. None of them knew what they were doing, but that didn't stop them. They were all good creatures and felt confident that good things happen to good creatures. (Although they had no evidence to support this rose-tinted belief...)

After twenty minutes of flapping and quackling, bleating and snorting, they were ready to go. Walli took off her hat and pulled out the bag with the disappearing spell, then handed it to Clifford. He stood on one of the kitchen chairs that he had placed by the cabinet and shook the spell over the top of it, trying to avoid any landing on him. The others watched as the spell, like a hand going into a glove, seemed to flow over the cabinet, covering every part of the outside.

Clifford climbed off the chair and put it to one side. Opening the door to the cabinet, he addressed his friends. "We need to go. Every second is precious."

Walli, Georgina and Reuben climbed into the cabinet. But Douglas didn't move.

Clifford looked at him. "What's the matter, Douglas? Aren't you coming?"

"I'm not sure that you've thought through this

rescue plan properly. I am naturally a cautious duck, and I can only help if there is absolute certainty that any rescue attempt will be successful. It was Aubrey's choice to put his neck on the line with the disappearing trick – and look what has happened to him. I am quite attached to my neck and therefore I'm not going to put it on any line."

"But, Douglas, how can I promise what will happen? None of us has done this before. We will need to take our chance and hope for the best."

The duck was far from convinced. "Tell me, Clifford, if you do manage to disappear, how do you know that you'll end up in the same place as Aubrey? And how do you know you will be able to get back?"

Clifford had given the matter a lot of thought on the way back from the Sisters' cave, and he had a ready answer for Douglas. "We can't be sure where we will go when we disappear. But we do know that Aubrey and Sol arrived in the same place when they disappeared, even though Aubrey vanished from this room and Sol from Cedilla on Sea, which is about a hundred kilometres away. And so I think there's a good chance that we'll end up in the same place as them. And as for us being able to reappear, the Sisters only became nasty after we had paid them and they had cast the spell. So I'm prepared to believe that the reappearing spell will work."

"This is all well and good," said Douglas, secretly irritated that Clifford's answer had been so well thought through, as this made it more difficult for the duck to duck out. "However, I don't need to tell you that in any rescue mission someone has to cover the rear. To make sure that no enemies can sneak up from behind. I am happy to take that important role, and the best place for me to play it is from this room. Also, I am claustrophobic and will probably faint if I get inside the cabinet. So, very reluctantly, I will stay behind. But you have my very best wishes and I hope to see you again soon!"

Clifford stared at Douglas. There was no point arguing with him, as Douglas was the most stubborn creature on the whole of Animaux.

"OK, see you later, Douglas," Clifford said, resting a friendly flipper on the duck's shoulder. Then Clifford joined the others inside the cabinet and closed the door behind him.

Douglas watched the cabinet intently. He could hear the muffled sound of Clifford saying the disappearing spell. And as soon as he had finished, the cabinet vanished.

The duck smiled, feeling very pleased with himself. He was sitting pretty. If none of his friends ever came back – and deep inside he was secretly, and wickedly, hoping they wouldn't – then he would have Aubrey's house all to himself. And he wouldn't share it with anyone. No, he would sell it and use the money to buy his ultimate dream – a banana plantation!

SCENE THREE – THE RETURN OF THE MELEAGRIS GALLOPAVO

The people-creature called Mick had spared Aubrey's life after dragging him back to the barn. But he put a tag on his leg, so Aubrey's name was now G801. From that moment on the turkey had kept a very low profile, mixing with all the other turkeys and staying close to Sol, who had crept back to the barn a few hours after Aubrey's forced return.

Aubrey had also become content to eat grain and drink water with the other turkeys. This had an unexpected benefit, as he lost quite a lot of weight. Of course, Aubrey still had no idea what the other turkeys were saying, and he didn't like the way he was pecked from time to time. But he didn't return any pecks he received; Aubrey was much too civilised for that. He didn't try to escape again. There was no point. Aubrey realised that he had seen Animaux for the last time, and he accepted this.

The weeks passed, until one morning there was more noise than usual outside the barn. Then the people-creatures called Mick and Phil entered through the small door.

Standing in the middle of the turkeys, Aubrey watched the people-creatures carefully, wondering what they were up to.

As usual, Phil entered the small office. He sat in the chair in front of the computer and called out to Mick. "I need to print out the shipping document. I'll just turn the computer and printer on and then we can get going."

"OK," said Mick. "But don't mess about on YouTube – we need to get this lot loaded on the trucks. The new ones are coming tomorrow and we've got a lot of cleaning to do before they arrive."

"I know, I know. It should only take a few minutes."

Aubrey broke away from the other turkeys and walked over to Sol, who was sitting on the wall about halfway down the barn.

"What's happening?" asked Aubrey.

Sol looked worried. "I've seen this before. This is when all the turkeys are loaded onto lorries and driven away. Oh Aubrey, I'm so sorry. I think this is it – the moment we've both been dreading for so many weeks."

Meanwhile Mick was laughing loudly as he walked over to the other turkeys, pointing to each one and saying, "Turkey burger tonight!"

There was a sudden commotion outside the barn. It sounded like one of the lorries had reversed into something. There was a lot of angry shouting and Phil and Mick went out to investigate.

"I don't want to go," gobbled Aubrey in great distress. "I am so afraid, Sol. Is there anything we can do?"

Although Sol didn't have any bright ideas, in a moment of sheer inspiration Aubrey suddenly came up with a plan. "I've got it! I've got a computer in my house. I know how they work. Perhaps I can press some buttons on the keyboard and stop them printing the shipping document. Then they won't be able to put us on the lorry."

"It's worth a try," said Sol, who didn't have the faintest idea how computers worked.

The two friends rushed into the office. Aubrey hopped up on the chair in front of the computer and looked at the screen, Sol as usual sitting on his shoulder. He flapped at the keyboard with his wings and a 'please enter your password' message appeared.

"What does this mean? What's the password?"

"I've no idea," said Sol. "Try turkey. Or barn. Or Five Wards."

Aubrey tried them all, plus a few others. But none worked and the 'please enter your password' message refused to go away.

The noise outside was dying down. It would only be a matter of time before Mick and Phil re-entered the barn.

In despair, Aubrey tried one last time to guess the password. But again he was incorrect. A tear rolled down his cheek and splashed onto the dusty floor below.

At precisely the same time, the ViciousVortex5 virus that had been dormant in Aubrey's brain for so long suddenly awoke as it sensed the presence of a new computer to infect. It wasted no time in invisibly sparkling out of Aubrey's left ear and crossing the gap between turkey and machine, to enter through one of the computer's USB ports. The virus rapidly infected the computer, causing it to crash.

"Great job, Aubrey – you've done it!" said Sol triumphantly, kissing the turkey on his tear-streaked cheek.

"Did I?" replied Aubrey, clueless about what had happened. "Yes, I did!"

The two friends ran out of the office, Aubrey pausing briefly to pick up and put on his cape, which the people-creature had thrown on the floor. Aubrey and Sol were only just in time, as Mick and Phil came back through the small barn door.

Phil walked back into the office. "What's wrong with the stupid computer? It's turned itself off and I can't turn it back on. That means that we can't print the shipping document!"

Mick had a reply that Aubrey didn't want to hear. "Don't worry, we can send it on later. We've done that before. Let's get these feathered things loaded. I could murder a cup of tea."

Phil left the office and opened the big barn door, walking outside. As soon as he had done so, Mick began to shoo the turkeys through the opening, up a ramp and into the back of a waiting lorry. Aubrey shrank away to the back of the barn, hoping that they might forget about him. But they didn't.

"Just the funny-coloured one left," said Mick, advancing towards him menacingly.

Aubrey knew that he couldn't win a fight with the people-creatures. All hope exited his body, to be replaced by dark, gnawing despair. If only he could conjure up a way out of the situation.

Conjure up! That was it!

"Sol, are you absolutely sure that none of the spells in your book work?"

Sol thought hard, very aware that the people-creature was closing on them fast. And then he remembered. "Wait a minute! I'd completely forgotten! When I bought the disappearing spell from the Weird Sisters, they were offering a BOGOF that day."

"What's a BOGOF?" asked Aubrey, surprised at what he thought was Sol being rude.

"It's short for Buy One Get One Free. They gave me a spell for slowing things down. Where's the book of spells?"

Aubrey pulled the book out from the cape's inner pocket and handed it to Sol. The salamander frantically thumbed through it.

"Where is it? I can't find it! I know I wrote it down when I got back to the Grand Theatre after visiting them. Hold on – there's two pages stuck together. I remember – I was eating a strawberry jam sandwich as I wrote the spell down. Some of the jam must have got on the page."

"Come here, turkey," Mick growled threateningly as he advanced on Aubrey. "And who put that cape on you again?"

Sol pulled the stuck pages apart and said in a clear voice:

"No need to hurry,
Don't tear around,
No cause to rush,
You must slow down."

The effect was instantaneous. Mick went into slow motion, going at only about 10% of his normal speed. But he was still walking towards Aubrey, closing in on him, a truly evil look on his face. He meant to do the turkey harm. And even if Aubrey dodged him, there was still Phil to contend with. This time, there would be no great escape for Aubrey the Turkey. He was about to gobble his last.

And then, as if by magic – in fact, certainly because of magic – the Cabinet of Esvaniss suddenly appeared behind Mick. The door was flung open and Clifford, Walli, Georgina and Reuben piled out. They spotted Aubrey straight away, and Clifford barked an order to Reuben.

"Reuben – take out that human!"

The ram obeyed without hesitation and gave Mick

an enormous butt on his backside. It sent him flying, still in slow motion, towards the barn wall.

The friends all came together. There was much hugging, tears, laughing and back-slapping. Aubrey proudly introduced Sol, and he was instantly accepted as an old and dear pal.

"So you got my message?" asked Aubrey, scarcely able to believe what was happening.

"Yes. Claude Crane Fly found it at Singsong Bay," replied Walli. "We'll tell you all about it when we get home."

"Home…" said Aubrey slowly. "HOME!" And he broke out into the most enormous smile. He had never imagined that this day would come. And now it was here, completely unexpected, and it tasted so very sweet!

"It's time to get going," said Clifford, who didn't want to stay in the barn a minute longer. "Everyone, get into the cabinet as quickly as possible and prepare to be tingled!"

"Tingled?" said Aubrey.

"Yes – the moment the cabinet disappeared, we all felt an odd tingling sensation all over our bodies. It was actually quite nice."

Another happy memory entered Aubrey's mind. "I remember! I felt the same thing when I disappeared. But it seems like such a long time ago."

As the friends filed into the cabinet, Phil, having finished talking to the lorry driver, came back into the barn in search of his colleague. He saw all the friends.

"What on earth is going on? Where did all these creatures come from, and who put that wardrobe there?"

And then he was rushing towards them, carrying a broom as a weapon and clearly intending to use it.

Needing no order this time, Reuben charged down the barn to slow down Phil. But the people-creature defended himself skilfully with his broom, knocking Reuben sideways and leaving him stunned.

"We've got to get going!" shouted Clifford. "Otherwise the humans will overpower us."

"But we can't leave Reuben!" screamed Georgina, and she galloped down the barn to help him. Being faster than the ram, Georgina was able to reach Phil before he could properly swing his broom. Horns down, she ran straight into his knees, causing him to tumble head over heels backwards, rather like a struck tenpin. Georgina helped the still dazed Reuben into the cabinet.

Clifford did a quick check. All the friends were safely inside the cabinet. It was time to go. They were homeward bound. As he closed the door, he noticed that the people-creatures had both recovered and were running towards the cabinet, shouting loudly.

"The spell had better work!" he thought, and then he said the magic words.

But he didn't feel a tingling feeling. He called out to the others to see if they had. The universal, worried answer was no. The Weird Sisters had tricked them! The reappearing spell didn't work! The people-creatures would get them!

And then the cabinet door was pulled open from outside. The friends closed their eyes and waited to be grabbed by the humans.

"Welcome back," quacked Douglas Duck. "Why have you all got your eyes closed?"

In the background was the unmistakable noise of the grandfather clock. It had started to tick again.

FOUR

THE DEAD SEA

Island of Animaux location:

» latitude 27° north

» longitude 135° west

As the morning sun rose slowly over Animaux, Clifford was slumped on the front doorstep of Aubrey's house, exhausted. He had not slept the previous night – in fact, he had not enjoyed a good night's sleep since Aubrey's rescue five days before. The platypus reckoned he must still be full of adrenaline after their escape from the turkey farm, and this meant he couldn't relax. In addition, a blistering heatwave had descended on Animaux three days ago, making life very uncomfortable. Daytime temperatures had reached 40°C in Wincot and were even hotter inland. At night it was equally uncomfortable, with no breeze and the temperature only dropping to a stifling 32°C.

The heatwave had caused chaos on the island. The government had officially declared a drought, and fresh water was rationed to one cup per creature per day. All tree shade was in short supply, with creatures appearing at dawn to reserve their places with towels, and some very selfishly not turning up to claim them until late morning. The swimming pool at Wincot Leisure Centre, an enormously popular place for overheated animals to cool down, had been put out of action for two weeks after a herd of overexcited hippopotamuses had dive-bombed all the other creatures and cracked the concrete pool base, allowing all the water to escape. And Georgina the Goat had experienced a huge demand for her ice cream. Her frantic attempts to meet it had resulted in her being admitted to hospital, suffering from acute dehydration and udder strain.

As Clifford stared vacantly down the garden path, Walli came out of the house and sat beside him.

"Howzit, Clifford. Didn't you sleep well again last night?" she asked, noticing how red and tired his eyes were looking. "It was really hot again, although I did manage to get some rest."

"G'day, Walli. No, I didn't sleep a wink," he replied. "I lay in bed for a long time, counting sheep then kangaroos then emus. But it was no good. I couldn't drift off. So, like I've been doing recently, I got up, came downstairs and came out into the garden. It's peaceful here at night, and the sky was clear. I was able to lie on the grass and look at the stars."

Walli nodded. She was worried about Clifford's insomnia, but she also had something else on her mind. It had been there ever since they had returned from the Isles of Scilly, and now it was time to share it with the platypus.

"Clifford, when we were rescuing Aubrey, were

you tempted to stay behind instead of coming back here?"

This had clearly also been on Clifford's mind. "Yes, I was tempted. Very tempted indeed."

"Then why didn't you stay, if you don't mind me asking?"

"No, I don't mind. I didn't think there was any point. I remembered from geography lessons at school that the Isles of Scilly are about as far away from Australia as it's possible to be. There's no way I could have swum home; it's much too far. So all that would have happened if I had stayed was that I wouldn't be home and I wouldn't be with Aubs and you and all my other friends here. So the decision was easy. I had to come back." Clifford turned to face her. "How about you? Did you think about staying?"

"A little bit. But the most important thing was to make sure that Aubrey was safe. And Sol. Now we know it's possible to leave Animaux, I'm sure we can find a way back home. Although for me that won't be through the hole I came out from under the gooseberry bush. I checked the other day, and it's vanished. I dug down a little way with my trotters but all I found was densely packed earth and stones. It's as if the hole had never existed."

"I know what you mean," said Clifford. "I've been down the toilet enough times, but it has never taken me back to Melbourne."

"Every day I miss my parents and my brothers and sisters more and more. I wonder if I will ever see them again."

"I'm sure you will, Walli. And until you do, I will always be here for you."

Walli gave Clifford a sweet smile. He was such a lovely friend. "Are you still worried about your mum?"

"Yes, very. She must be so upset, wondering what has happened to me. Luckily my aunt lives nearby, so I guess my mum will have been spending time with her."

"If you don't mind me asking, what happened to your dad?"

"It's OK to ask. He left when I was very little. I don't really remember him. I do know that he made Mum very sad. She told me he had gone walkabouts with a younger lady platypus. They had settled down, even had kids. So I've got some half-brothers and half-sisters somewhere, although I've never met them. And I never saw my dad again."

"Perhaps when you finally get back to Australia you can try and find him?"

"Not after what he did to Mum. Anyway, there's no chance. We heard four years ago that he'd been eaten by a dingo."

The two friends sat in silence, Walli thinking that Clifford's dad's fate was very similar to her Uncle Narciso's.

Suddenly Clifford gave a huge yawn. He stretched, then shifted, to ease the numbness in his bottom that had been caused by sitting for too long without moving, and gently flicked his tail from side to side.

"Walli, there's something very odd about this island."

"What do you mean? That it's full of animals but has no humans?"

"There is that. But there's something else. You remember how interested I am in science? Well, that includes astronomy. You know – star gazing and planet watching?"

"Yes, you've told me about the planets before. How they orbit around the sun and how some are made of rock while others are made of ice and gas. And that all the stars we can see in the night sky are just other suns, some of which may have their own planets going around them."

"That's right. Because the Earth spins from side to side and not from top to bottom, we can see stars in Australia and South Africa that can't be seen if you live in the northern half of the planet. So we can see the stars that make up the Southern Cross, and the Magellanic Clouds. And creatures in the northern part of the planet can see the North Star, Polaris, and the Little Bear constellation which it is in."

Walli nodded. "I understand that. And you've reminded me that I need to look at the stars more often. But do you mean that there's something odd about the stars we can see from Animaux?"

Clifford smiled at Walli. She was a very clever warthog, and as usual she had understood the point he was making.

"Bullseye, my good friend. Bullseye. During the nights I've spent in the garden over the last few days, and over the last few months, I've seen stars from all over the sky. So one night I saw the Southern Cross, the next night I saw the Little Bear, and the night after

I saw the stars that lie between the two, which must mean we are near the equator. But that's crazy – it's just not possible for the stars to move about like they have been doing. So there's only one possible answer."

"What's that?" asked Walli, thinking perhaps that the Earth had suddenly started to spin from top to bottom, even though Clifford said it didn't.

"I think that somehow the Island of Animaux is moving around the planet. So one day it's south of the equator, the next day north and so on. That might also be why the weather is so changeable, never the same from day to day."

"But how is that possible? Islands can't just move on their own, can they?"

"I've never heard of it before. But as we've already agreed, this is a strange island. Perhaps it's got giant propellers somewhere that move it just like a ship."

The friends thought about this for a few moments. Walli reckoned it was more likely to be a giant sail that was moving the island, as it seemed unlikely that the creatures who lived on Animaux could have built the giant engine that would be needed to drive such propellers.

"In the last few days, something new has

happened," continued Clifford. "The island has stopped moving – the stars have been the same each night. And so, at least for the moment, we seem to be stuck somewhere on Earth."

"Can you tell where?" asked Walli.

"Looking at all the stars, I'm pretty certain that we're north of the equator. But we must be either in or close to the Tropic of Cancer – the heatwave we're stuck in confirms that."

"Can we do anything to get the island moving again?"

"I don't think so. Remember, I didn't even suspect it was moving until recently. Perhaps things will return to normal soon. Although it's also possible that being in one place is normal and all the moving was odd. Animaux is such a strange place – anything is possible."

Once again the friends sat in silence. The rising sun shone warmly on their faces.

"Talking about strange things, how's Aubs today? Was he awake when you got up?"

"Yes. I went in to see him. He was snuggled in bed and said he'd had a lovely sleep, despite the heat. I made him a cup of tea and some toast. And then he asked for seconds! His appetite is definitely returning, which is just as well considering how much weight he lost when he was at the turkey farm."

Clifford nodded. "It's good to see the old Aubs slowly coming back. Including the size of his belly! And it's great to have him home. He's being much nicer to us now than he was before his magic trick went wrong. I wonder how long it will last."

"Let's go upstairs and see him. And if he asks for more food, you can make the tea and toast this time!"

Walli and Clifford got up and entered the house.

But there was no need for them to climb the stairs to see Aubrey, as he was sitting in his armchair, wearing pyjamas, a dressing gown and bunny rabbit slippers. Plus the new bobble hat that Martha had knitted for him as a 'coming home' present. He must have been nearly melting in the heat.

"Hello, my flippered and trottered pals. Have you been enjoying the nice morning? I thought you might have been in the kitchen, preparing a third delicious breakfast for me, to help me celebrate."

Walli and Clifford rolled their eyes then looked at the turkey, who was clearly feeling very pleased with himself. Aubrey had cast the line with his 'celebrate' comment, and they knew he was waiting for one of them to bite. Walli decided it was her turn.

"It's lovely to see you up at last, Aubrey, after being in bed for the past four days. Is that what you are celebrating?"

"Nope. Not even warm."

The warthog tried again. "Is it because you managed to sell the Cabinet of Esvaniss and book of spells to Sol, even though the three gold eagles he paid was half what you paid Geraldine?"

"Another miss, Walli. Let me explain. We've all

had a difficult time recently, what with me being away and you trying everything to get me back, putting yourselves in great danger in the process. And so I've decided that we all deserve some R&R."

Walli looked puzzled. "What's R&R? Is that rhubarb and then more rhubarb? I'm not sure I want that, as I think it will give me tummy ache."

"Not rhubarb, Walli. R&R is short for 'rest and recuperation'. I saw it on the Turkeynet. Apparently, people-creatures who are soldiers like to do it. Let me put it another way – I think we all deserve a holiday."

Seeing the chance to wear sunglasses and smother himself in sun cream, Clifford was very enthusiastic. "Nice one, Aubs! I couldn't agree more. Lying by a cool pool with an even cooler drink nearby. Being fussed over by other creatures and having a really lazy time. I'm in!"

Walli, being very practical, felt that some more details were necessary. "It does sound nice. But where will we go on holiday? Or did you mean that we would have a holiday here?"

Aubrey smiled at her. "Not here, Walli. When I was little my parents used to take my sister and me to Cedilla on Sea. It has a beautiful sandy beach and the sea is as blue as the sky. And of course there's the grand pier with the theatre at the end, where Sol performed. When we went we stayed in a guest house, but this time I think we should spoil ourselves. And so we shall be staying at the Cedilla Charlton, the finest hotel on the whole of Animaux!"

"Do you mean that you have booked the hotel already?" asked Clifford.

"Yes!" gobbled Aubrey in high excitement. "I phoned the Cedilla Charlton and made the booking just before you came in. That's why I'm celebrating. We're going on holiday!"

With that Aubrey stood up and, perhaps for the first time in his life, did a little jig. Walli and Clifford joined him, and soon the friends were joyously spinning around the front room, occasionally colliding with each other and eventually collapsing in a dizzy, laughing heap.

"When will our holiday start?" asked Walli when her dizziness had begun to clear.

"Straight away," replied Aubrey. "I have booked our rooms from tonight for one whole week. I suggest we have some breakfast, pack our things and then head to the railway station to catch the train to Cedilla on Sea."

"How long is the train ride, Aubs?"

"About eight hours."

"Strewth, that's a long time. It would almost be quicker if we walked."

"It's because the steam engine that pulls the train is very old. In fact, it was the first one that was ever built. It's going to be replaced next year and will be moved to the Transportation Museum in Brusdor, where it will be put on display. The new train service will only take one hour, so a huge improvement."

The friends enjoyed a big breakfast, chattering excitedly about what they would do in Cedilla on Sea and agreeing to have competitions to see who could eat the most ice cream and drink the most red lemonade. Aubrey was confident he would win both.

Clifford and Walli didn't have too much to pack. However, Aubrey decided to take all his clothes, pillows, and twelve kilos of acorns. He just about managed to squeeze everything in his battered old suitcase, the only one he owned, and had Clifford sit on the lid so he could press the two catches to close it.

"There's only one train per day to Cedilla on Sea. We need to get going if we're going to catch it," said Aubrey. "Clifford, would you mind carrying my suitcase to the door? I'm still feeling a little weak after my recent adventure."

"A little weak, a lot lazy," mumbled the platypus as he dragged the heavy case across the floor.

Aubrey phoned Douglas and asked him to meet them at the station. The duck could look after Aubs' skateboard until they returned.

"Walli, Clifford – my legs are too wobbly for me to stand on the skateboard. So you will need to carry me on it."

"You've got to be kidding, Aubs. How are we supposed to do that?"

"Must I do all your thinking for you, Clifford?" replied Aubrey, slipping smoothly into the role of teacher.

Clifford gave him a glare. He was prepared to cut the turkey some slack because of his recent awful experience, but he felt that Aubrey was starting to take advantage of the situation.

"All right, Aubs, we'll do it, but just this once. What you're asking us to do is very dangerous, as we will have real difficulty controlling the skateboard. Walli, I'll lay the suitcase flat on the skateboard. You get on the back and sit upright, holding out your front trotters. I'll do the same on the front, holding my flippers out and facing you. Aubs, you sit on our trotters and flippers and try not to squirm around too much."

The three friends went outside and took their positions, ending up looking like a troupe of performing circus acrobats. Then Clifford leant back slightly, shifting the skateboard's centre of gravity and causing it to start to roll forward. It quickly gathered pace and the platypus skilfully steered it through the garden gate and down Fluffy Cloud Lane, using a mixture of well-timed body sways and very nervous backward glances.

After a truly terrifying ride they rolled to a halt outside the magnificent red-brick front of Wincot Railway Station. Douglas was waiting from them.

"Thanks for agreeing to look after the skateboard," said Aubrey as he clambered off the exhausted Walli and Clifford. "No time to talk now, but we'll be back in a week. I'll phone to tell you when."

Aubrey strode into the station, his wobbly legs having apparently recovered. Walli and Clifford followed, after giving Douglas friendly smiles. The platypus dragged the suitcase with heavy, aching flippers.

"Wait here, I'll get the tickets," Aubrey shouted and went off to find the counter.

An exhausted Walli and Clifford sat on the suitcase and waited for him. All around them were the sounds of guards blowing whistles to announce train departures and the *chuff-chuff*ing of steam trains pulling out from the station.

"We deserve a holiday after that ride," reflected Clifford. "And there's no way that we're going to carry him home when we get back!"

Walli nodded in agreement. She was then distracted by a billboard. It carried the headline from that day's edition of the *Animaux Times*.

CRISIS FOR ANIMAUX. HAS THE END COME? screamed the headline.

"What crisis do you think that is, Clifford? It doesn't sound very good."

"I don't know, Walli. I haven't been keeping up with the news recently." He noticed Aubrey rushing back with three tickets in his wing.

"Do you know what the crisis is, Aubs?"

"The only crisis is that if we don't hurry we will miss our train. It's about to leave from Platform 2!"

The friends rushed towards the platform, Walli and Clifford carrying the suitcase between them. They passed Rick Rat, who was standing at the platform entrance, a big smile on his whiskery face. Animals appeared to be dropping coins into a bucket he was holding. But the three friends didn't have time to stop and see what he was up to, tumbling aboard the train just before it pulled away.

SCENE TWO – HAPPY HOLIDAY

The carriage they were travelling in was truly ancient. There were no comfortable padded seats;

instead there were only backless wooden benches to sit on.

"Aubs, where's the toilet?" asked Clifford. "I meant to go at the station but there wasn't time."

"There isn't one. Most creatures go out of the window. You might find a bucket at the far end, if you're lucky."

"What about food, Aubrey? Is there a snack trolley service?"

"I'm afraid not, Walli. That's why I brought acorns. I was surprised that you and Clifford didn't bring anything to eat or drink, given that it's an eight-hour journey."

"We didn't know the service would be this basic," replied Clifford, heading off to the end of the carriage to look for a bucket.

Walli settled on a bench, looking out of the window at the passing countryside. Aubrey sat beside her, having opened his case and taken out a wingful of acorns.

"Care for one of these, Walli?" he asked, holding out one that looked rotten.

"No, thank you, Aubrey. But it was kind of you to offer."

Clifford returned. "That's better. You were right about there being a bucket, Aubs. But they should empty it more often. By the way, guess what I've just seen?"

"In the bucket?"

"No, not there. You see those two creatures sitting on the bench down there, facing the other way?"

"Yes. What of them?"

"Well, either I've gone mad or they are a couple of dodos."

"Dodos?" said a surprised Walli. "You mean those large flightless birds that used to live on the island of Mauritius and that have been extinct for ages?"

"The exact same, mate."

"I don't know where Mauritius is," began Aubrey. "But there are plenty of dodos on Animaux. In fact, there's a big colony of them in Cedilla on Sea. I don't mean to be unkind, but they're not the cleverest birds on the island."

"And who is the cleverest, Aubs?" asked Clifford, pulling the turkey's leg.

"Excluding me, it's probably Elizabeth Eagle."

Clifford winked at Walli and they smiled. Old big-head was back!

Sara Squirrel, the train guard, suddenly appeared from nowhere. She checked their tickets, as usual franking them with her teeth. Sara told them she would be back every twenty minutes to check the tickets, "just in case". She then disappeared out of the window and scampered onto the carriage roof, after having secretly stuffed four of Aubrey's acorns in her coin bag.

The train puffed along, *click-clack*ing down the track. Occasionally smoke and hot, gritty cinders blew in through the open carriage window. The friends brushed them away, tears flowing when a cinder landed in their eyes.

Then they were distracted by the two dodos, who had begun to talk very loudly to each other.

"It's a crisis," said the first.

"Yes, a crisis, no question about it," said the second.

"Quite dreadful."

"Agreed – awful."

"You mean both dreadful and awful, at the same time?"

"I do. And I might go so far as to say it's terrible."

"Dreadful, awful and terrible? Do you really mean it? Wow – that's really serious."

"I mean all three. And 'serious' as well, since you threw that in."

Clifford got up and went to talk to the dodos. "Excuse me, mates. I couldn't help overhearing you just now. When we were at the station, we saw a headline that said Animaux was in crisis. Is that what you were talking about?"

"It is," said the second dodo.

"May I ask what the crisis is? I haven't kept up with the news recently."

"It's a dreadful crisis," said the first.

"I'm sure it is, but can you provide more details?" asked the platypus.

"It is a crisis that is both dreadful and awful," said the second.

"Dreadful, awful and terrible," said the first. The second nodded in agreement.

"And serious?" asked Clifford, realising that the dodos would never get to the point.

"Exactly!" said the dodos together.

Clifford turned his back on the dodos and trudged back to Walli and Aubrey, as they added the word 'shocking' to their list.

"Aubs, for once I agree with you. Dodos are not the cleverest birds."

It was dark when the train pulled into Cedilla on Sea. The friends left their carriage, leaving the two dodos behind. They were terribly excited, having just thought of the word 'appalling' to add to their list.

The station was deserted and there were no taxis outside, so the friends decided to walk to the Cedilla Charlton. Aubrey promised that it was only five minutes away.

After thirty minutes, they arrived. Walli and Clifford were a little cross, both with Aubrey's bad directions and because he hadn't offered to help them carry his suitcase. But they cheered up when they saw the hotel. It looked very luxurious, and they couldn't wait to check in and go to their comfortable rooms.

SCENE THREE – ROOM WITHOUT A VIEW

Aubrey walked to the front desk and completed the formalities. After a few minutes he came back, holding out a single key.

"This is for your room. It's in the basement, next to the boiler room. It might be a little hot and noisy, and there's no window. But it's all they had left, since I booked so late."

Both friends were very disappointed, but they decided not to show it. After all, Aubrey had been kind enough to book the holiday.

"Is your room near ours, Aubrey?" asked Walli.

"Of course not. I'm on the top floor, in the Presidential Suite. It's got three bedrooms, living and dining rooms, a Jacuzzi and a huge outside terrace with a sea view. And best of all, it has twenty-four-hour butler service!"

"Hang on, mate," Clifford began. "Why do we need

to stay in the dungeon and you get the best room in the hotel? Aren't we all supposed to be having a nice holiday?"

"With the saving I made on your room, I was able to spend more on mine," replied Aubrey. "Clifford, I deserve this holiday more than anyone. So don't be ungrateful. Or greedy. Remember, this is a free holiday for you. Anyway, you'll forget all about the room when you're sunbathing on the beach."

As Clifford simmered with rage, Walli tried a gentler approach. "Aubrey, your room has three bedrooms. Couldn't we have one each? That would mean we'll all be together, and that would be nice."

Aubrey looked at her-somewhat coldly, she felt. "I'm afraid not, Walli. I plan to sleep in all of them each night. Two hours in one, three hours in the second, three hours in the third. I will ask the butler to wake me when it's time to move. I'll probably ask him to carry me from bed to bed and tuck me in."

Aubrey then surprised them by giving them a warm smile. "I'll tell you what. Why don't you join me on my terrace tomorrow morning for breakfast? I'll ask my butler to prepare something. Come at 6am, just as the sun is rising. Then we'll be able to look at the sandy beach and beautiful blue sea. I'll leave my bedroom door ajar, so walk right in. But now I need my sleep, so goodnight to both of you."

Aubrey turned and strode towards the lift, gesturing to a dodo bellboy to carry his suitcase for him. Walli and Clifford watched him go.

"Let's look on the bright side, Clifford. We're in a lovely hotel by the sea. The weather is fantastic and we've got a tasty breakfast to look forward to tomorrow. Things aren't that bad, are they?"

"You're right, Walli. Let's have a great time. It's nice of Aubs to treat us."

As they walked towards the stairs that led down to the basement, Clifford briefly chatted to the dodo who was on duty at the check-in desk. The dodo confirmed that the crisis was dreadful, awful and terrible. But said no more.

Walli's and Clifford's room was even more basic than they had feared. It was hot, very noisy and small, and the two beds were narrow and uncomfortable. It did not have an en suite, so they had to go back up to reception to use the bathroom. But since they were so tired after their long day, they slept very well.

Before going to sleep, Walli had set her internal

alarm clock for 5.50am. It sounded on time, and she woke Clifford. They walked to reception, then boarded the lift to visit Aubrey.

As promised, Aubrey had left the door to his suite – the only one on the top floor – open. They entered and called out to him and he answered from his terrace.

"I'm out here. Come quickly, the sun is about to rise. Have a drink and sit next to me. You're about to see one of the most beautiful sights on the whole of Animaux."

Walli and Clifford rushed to sit on the large sofa next to Aubrey. He was looking very comfortable, wearing a fluffy white towelling robe and nibbling a buttered croissant. He handed them each a glass of delicious, fresh orange juice.

The friends looked out to sea. The mist that usually surrounded the island had vanished, and they could see the first rays of sun appear above the horizon. As the sun continued to rise, its rays lengthened, rushing towards Animaux. And the rays began to illuminate the sea and sand. But the rays did not turn the sea blue and the sand gold. Instead, they had a strange translucent sheen, as if they were covered by the same thing. Aubrey gobbled in surprise, unsure what he was seeing. Clifford got up and walked to the edge of the balcony. He strained his eyes to see what was covering the sea and the sand. And then he knew.

"Plastic! Plastic! The whole of the sea and beach is covered in plastic waste! Plastic waste made by humans! Look what they have done to the environment – see the impact it has had on beautiful Animaux! Look at the dead sea, the dead beach! When will humans learn? When will they stop destroying the planet?"

FIVE

SEA OF GREEN

Island of Animaux location:
- » latitude 27° north
- » longitude 135° west

Clifford rushed from Aubrey's suite down to the beach, his two friends close behind. When he arrived, things were even worse than the platypus feared. A huge amount of debris, consisting of all types of plastic packaging, fishing lines and general waste, covered the beach and water as far as the eye could see.

Clifford, Walli and Aubrey stood together. This was a nightmare that none of them could ever have imagined.

"Help me!" came a strangled cry. Clifford looked to his right and was horrified to see a sea turtle with the loop from a plastic six-pack ring, used to hold drinks cans together, around its neck. He ran over and stretched the loop with his front flippers so that he could pull it over the turtle's head.

"Thank you ever so much," said the grateful turtle. "I've had that around my neck since yesterday evening and I couldn't get it off. I thought I was going to be strangled."

"Do you know how long the plastic has been here, mate? Is this the crisis that the *Animaux Times* reported?"

"It's called plastic, is it? No one around here knows what it is. Yes, it's what the newspaper reported. The problem started four days ago. This plastic stuff appeared overnight all around the island, at the same time that the heatwave started. So many poor creatures have suffered horrible fates. I've seen gulls eating plastic bags and whales eating empty bottles, mistaking them for food. The hospitals are full to overflowing with the desperately sick, and the doctors and nurses don't know what to do."

Walli and Aubrey joined them.

"Is the government doing anything?" the turkey asked.

"They're saying that everything is under control and things will soon return to normal. But they're not saying how, and last night His Holiness the Hooded Ganglia said we're all heading for Judgement Day.

President Elizabeth Eagle has been touring all the coastal towns to assess the scale of the problem for herself and to provide comfort where she can. She was in Shellville yesterday and she's due here later this morning. She will be holding a meeting with the press and local creatures in the conference room at the Cedilla Charlton hotel."

A group of dodos wandered by, all agreeing that the crisis was dreadful, awful and terrible.

The three friends decided to return to Aubrey's suite, realising there was nothing more they could do about the plastic. There, they sat sadly on the terrace, eating their breakfast in silence.

Finally Clifford spoke. "I can't believe we didn't know this had happened! All we needed to do was read the paper or turn on the TV."

Aubrey looked at him. "But even if we had known earlier, what could we have done?"

"Fair point, Aubs. Has anything like this ever happened before?"

"Not in my lifetime. We've had some bad storms, but they didn't affect the whole island. And the government always had a plan to make things better."

"Have you any idea what has happened, Clifford?"

asked Walli, hoping that her friend could provide an answer.

Clifford thought for a few moments. He hoped what he was going to say didn't sound crazy. "Walli, remember when we were in the garden yesterday morning and I said that the stars weren't changing any more? And that it must be because Animaux had stopped moving? Let's suppose the plastic has somehow stopped Animaux from moving."

"But how is that possible? Surely plastic can't stop something as big as an island?"

"Well, it depends how the island moves in the first place. And how much plastic there is. From my science studies, I know there are places on Earth where the oceans are covered by great patches of plastic rubbish. Thanks to humans. Perhaps we've got stuck in one of those patches."

"Do you really think so? Do you know which patch we are stuck in?"

"I can't be sure. As I mentioned yesterday, I think we're north of the equator, but not that far north. So, as an educated guess I'd say that we could be in the eastern section of the Great Pacific Garbage Patch, which floats between Hawaii and the west coast of America."

Aubrey had been listening carefully. He hadn't been able to contribute much because he didn't know enough about the world outside Animaux, despite his unplanned stay in the Scilly Isles. Now he spoke up.

"I think we should attend the President's meeting. She knows me a little bit because I once invited her to my dinner party. She didn't accept and I'm still cross with her. But I could introduce you to her, Clifford. I'm sure she'd be interested to hear your theory."

"Aubs, there are very few creatures on Animaux who know that a world exists beyond it. If I start speaking about rubbish patches off the coast of America, then the Crow police will arrest me for being insane!"

Aubrey put a comforting wing on Clifford's shoulder. "Given the crisis, I'm sure that Elizabeth would be willing to listen to anyone who could explain what has happened."

Aubrey was talking sense. Clifford had information that no one else could know. He had to share it.

The friends finished their breakfast then stood looking over the balcony at the chaotic scene below.

The President's meeting started at 10am in the main conference room on the ground floor. Aubrey,

Clifford and Walli arrived early and got front-row seats. The room was soon packed.

Elizabeth Eagle appeared exactly on time. She stood on the small stage at the front of the room, ready to address the crowd. She was flanked by Crow police officers, led by the sinister Chief of Police, Carinus Crow. Unusually for a crow, Carinus had grey feathers. He also wore a monocle.

The crows ran their beady eyes over every creature in the room, looking for any that might cause trouble. Walli felt particularly uncomfortable with the intense looks they gave her.

Clifford and Walli had only ever seen Elizabeth Eagle on postage stamps and coins. In reality, she was magnificent. She was tall, with a bright yellow beak and white plumes on her head. Elizabeth's body was covered in dark brown feathers and her tail feathers were white. On her feet she wore elegant, pointed shoes.

She looked ahead and spoke clearly and calmly to the packed audience. "Dear fellow creatures, I must be truthful to everyone here. This is a moment of great crisis for the Island of Animaux. We have been surrounded by a strange substance and, despite the

best efforts of our scientists, we haven't been able to identify it. And we do not know where it has come from. It has caused great injury to many creatures, and to the economy of our wonderful island."

There were gasps in the room, and some angry snorts. Elizabeth held up her wings to restore order. "Fellow creatures, please try to remain calm. Your government will deal with the problem. And don't forget about the island-wide competition that was launched two days ago. Creatures are invited to call a special number and make suggestions for how the substance can be cleared. The best idea will be rewarded with 1,000 gold eagles. There's still time to make the call, and we hope to announce the winner at lunchtime."

There were more gasps in the room, accompanied by some greedy clucks and cackles.

A dodo journalist called out a question to Elizabeth. "Is the crisis dreadful?"

"It is," she replied.

Another dodo journalist took its chance. "Is the crisis awful?"

"It is," she replied.

A third dodo journalist shouted out. "Is the crisis terrible?"

"It's that as well," replied Elizabeth, wondering when she would be asked a sensible question.

Clifford decided that it was time for him to speak. He held up his flipper to attract her attention.

Elizabeth saw him, relieved that he wasn't a dodo. "Good morning. What would you like to say?"

The platypus nervously cleared his throat. He had never addressed a president before. Or spoken in front of such a large crowd. "Madam President. I come from Australia, a land far beyond this island. The substance you mentioned is called plastic, and it is waste created by humans. It floats in great patches on all the oceans of the Earth, and I believe that Animaux has become stuck in one of those patches."

As he finished speaking, the room erupted. Creatures shrieked, hissed and growled at him. There were deafening howls and squawks – both at the nonsense they assumed he had just spoken and his disrespect in saying it to the President.

Carinus advanced threateningly to the front of the stage. "Plastic – what is that? And humans – what are they? Australia – nonsense! The Earth – rubbish!" Frantically, he gestured to his officers. "Team – he's mad. Just the way he looks confirms that, with that funny bill and flippers. He's clearly dangerous and might be armed. Get him before he does something wicked!"

Before Clifford had the chance to move, twenty Crow police had swooped down and began to peck him mercilessly.

"STOP!" shouted Elizabeth. "Leave him alone. He is not dangerous and he must not be hurt. Officers, I command you to return to your stations immediately."

With a few grumbled caws the Crow police obeyed her. Carinus tried to have a word, but she waved him away. Elizabeth looked at Clifford warmly. "I would

like to have a private discussion with you after this meeting. Do you have time?"

Relieved that the assault was over, Clifford couldn't answer quickly enough. "Of course, mate – sorry, Madam President. I'd be happy to chat. We can use the Presidential Suite, if you like? My mate Aubs has booked it, and I'm sure he wouldn't mind."

Aubrey nodded furiously. If he played his cards right, he might be able to persuade Elizabeth to have a selfie taken with him. He'd long coveted that. He could then show the selfie to all the other creatures, especially the Cloaked Croak, to prove that he was best pals with the President.

Elizabeth turned her attention back to the audience. "Fellow creatures, as your President, I want to assure you that we will be OK. It may take some time, and so I ask for your patience. But we will emerge from this crisis stronger than before. Thank you."

A huge cheer went up, and all creatures present applauded, using their hooves, wings, paws, pincers or whatever else they had available. Elizabeth was the most popular leader in the whole of Animaux's history, and the creatures loved her.

Smiling, she waved at the audience then left the stage, gesturing to Clifford to follow her. Aubrey and Walli tagged along, keen not to miss out on the private meeting.

Elizabeth exited the conference room and strode through the hotel reception, heading for the lift. She was quickly joined by Carinus, who continued to look suspiciously at Clifford. They were also accompanied by the joint chief scientists of Animaux, Bernyce Bonobo and Orlando Owl, dressed in white doctors' coats.

The group squeezed into the lift. Elizabeth pressed the button to the floor of the Presidential Suite. "I always stay in the suite when I'm in town. It was nice of them to name it after me. It's a beautiful room, although at ten gold eagles per night I think the hotel charges far too much for it."

Clifford and Walli looked at each other. The room would cost Aubrey seventy gold eagles for the week! Where would he get the money from? He had the three eagles that Sol had given him. That meant that he was sixty-seven eagles short. No doubt he would expect Clifford and Walli to work hard for many weeks to pay the rest!

SCENE TWO – THE BIGGEST SECRETS EVER

The lift stopped on the top floor and the group entered the suite.

"Let's sit in the lounge," said Elizabeth. "It's the best place for the meeting."

Clifford, Aubrey and Walli squashed together on the sofa, which was much smaller than the one on the balcony. Elizabeth sat in an armchair, with the chief scientists and Carinus standing beside her. She looked at the platypus.

"Clifford, you spoke about plastic and humans. Neither of those words exists on Animaux. What did you mean?"

Clifford thought it was time for some straight

talking. "Elizabeth, if you don't mind me calling you by your first name, I don't come from Animaux. I arrived by accident from Australia. My friend Walli arrived by accident from South Africa. There is a big world beyond this island, and that's where we come from."

Elizabeth nodded, as if she knew what Clifford was talking about. This surprised him, but he continued. "Human beings are the dominant creatures on every part of the Earth – apart from this island. There's lots of them. They can be nice, but some of them create lots of trouble. And they all produce loads of rubbish. Some of this ends up in the sea, and that was what I mentioned in the meeting downstairs."

It was Elizabeth's turn to speak. "I know there is a world beyond this island. And I know about humans. But there are very few other creatures on Animaux, beyond the ones in this room, who also know about them. As President, it is my duty to make sure this doesn't change. The creatures of Animaux must continue to believe that there is nowhere to live other than this island."

"I don't understand, Elizabeth. Why shouldn't they know?"

"Many centuries ago, the Animaux elders decided they wanted to keep the island as the last place on Earth where humans were not present. They saw the enormous impact that humans have had on the planet, and their need to constantly explore new places and change them when they got there. Sea birds reached Animaux with these stories. I am fearful that if the creatures on Animaux found out about humans, they would panic. This would lead to dangerous stampedes, putting lives at risk."

"What did the elders do to prevent the people-creatures from coming?" asked Aubrey, excited that he was about to learn something that wasn't taught in school.

Elizabeth turned to Bernyce Bonobo, indicating that she should explain.

"The best scientists and engineers dug out a huge cavern beneath the Great Plunder Plain. In that space they installed a high-acceleration linear motor. The motor, using positive and negative magnetic forces, can move the island, at enormous speed, to any place on the planet. Because it is so big, the motor makes the ground vibrate and makes a humming noise. To prevent it from being discovered, stories were made up to scare creatures and stop them from visiting the Great Plunder Plain. Dreadful creatures were said to live there, including acid-spitting scarab beetles, screaming hairy trotter-splitters, nose-less magnetic beak grabbers and bad-tempered fire ants. How clever the elders were!"

"The trotter-splitters really do exist! I saw them," said Walli, remembering her visit to Black Rock.

"Me too," said Aubrey and Clifford together.

Elizabeth looked at them, puzzled. She took over from Bernyce. "And so every night the island is moved to a new place, to reduce the chance of humans finding us. If we remain in the same place, then there is a chance that we will eventually be discovered."

Bernyce added some more details. "The motor also allows us to create an artificial sea fog. We use this to cloak the island so it can't be seen from the sea or air."

"This is fascinating," quackled Clifford, greatly enjoying the science lesson. "But why has the island stopped moving?"

It was Orlando Owl's turn to explain. "The linear motor requires huge amounts of sea water to keep it cool. Water is collected using giant inlet valves situated around the coast. However, each one is blocked with this … plastic, as you call it. No sooner do we clear it out than it washes back and clogs things up again. We've had to shut down the motor to prevent it from overheating and exploding."

Elizabeth summarised the situation. "And so you see our problem. We are stuck, and the sea fog shield is down. I am greatly concerned that humans will find us at last and invade. If that happens, it will be the end of the Island of Animaux as we know it."

"Elizabeth, I said earlier that some humans cause trouble. But many are very nice. If they do discover the island, then it might not be as bad as you think."

"We know what it will be like. You see, humans have already visited Animaux."

If the three friends hadn't been sitting down, they would have fallen flat on their backs, so surprised and shocked were they by the unexpected news.

"I can't believe it," said Aubrey. "When did this happen? Are they still here? Will they want to live in my house? Because I don't have enough room."

Elizabeth smiled at him. "They are not here any longer and I think your house is safe. It all happened a long time ago."

"How long ago?" asked Walli, hoping that when she grew up she would be as clever as Elizabeth.

"It was about one hundred and forty years ago, long before any of us was born. But Godfrey the Giant Tortoise remembers. Giant tortoises live for so long, and at the time Godfrey was a thirty-five-year-old school teacher in Brusdor."

Aubrey couldn't believe what he was hearing. He had never imagined that Godfrey was once young, thinking of him only as an elderly, short-sighted, rather silly tortoise who liked to collect stamps. What a secret Godfrey had been keeping! Aubrey now had deep respect for the tortoise.

"One morning a gull spotted a group of humans on the beach near Brusdor. They had landed in a rowing boat, had got out and were lying on the sand, exhausted. The president at the time, Esteban Eagle, ordered the Armadillo Army, accompanied by some gorillas from the Pluie Rain Forest, who acted as bodyguards, to round them up and take them to the north wing of the Presidential Palace."

"How many humans were there?" asked Aubrey.

"Ten. Eight were male and two were female. One of the females was a two-year-old child."

"What happened when they arrived at the palace?" said Clifford.

"The humans behaved well, for a while. The gorillas made sure of that, before returning to the forest. We gave them fruit and vegetables to eat, water to drink and a place to rest. Most of the time they looked at us as if they couldn't believe what they were seeing. Perhaps they hadn't seen free, educated creatures before. We tried to talk to them, but they didn't understand us. Although, strangely, the little girl did, even though she was still learning to talk. Perhaps human children have abilities that most lose when they grow up. But even when she got older, the girl could always talk with us."

"I had the same problem with the Mick and Phil people-creatures not understanding me when I was on the turkey farm," said Aubrey, then wished he hadn't because Elizabeth wouldn't know what he was talking about and would probably think him silly. But she didn't seem to notice his remark.

"Do you know where the humans came from?" asked Walli.

"Yes. One of the men, who was dressed in a smart uniform and who wore a special cap during the day, kept writing things in a book. One night when he was asleep, three mice managed to remove it and take it to Esteban. He read it and found that the man in the uniform was named Captain Benjamin Briggs and the woman was his wife, Sarah. The child was their daughter, Sophia. The other men were Captain Briggs' crew."

Elizabeth caught her breath. "They were on a ship called the *Mary Celeste*, which was carrying cargo from New York to Genoa, Italy. Captain Briggs wrote that they had just passed Santa Maria Island in the Azores when they saw a strange island surrounded by fog. It wasn't on the map, so Briggs decided they should explore it – and possibly claim it for America. Everyone boarded a rowing boat and headed for the island, which of course was Animaux. I've checked the island movement records, and on the day the humans were found on the beach, Animaux's location was latitude 37° north, longitude 24° west."

Walli was concerned about the humans' welfare, especially Sophia's. "Did they all remain on the island?"

"No. In fact, things ended very sadly. First, the crew started to misbehave. They were being guarded by a rooster and a swan. The crew started to pull faces at the guards and clap their hands to frighten them. One morning the crew and the guards went missing. The men were found at the back of the palace, where they had lit a fire. On the ground were bones and plucked feathers. They had obviously eaten the poor rooster and swan! The gorillas were called, but the men ran off before they arrived. They were chased but ran into the Deadly Bottomless Swamp. The men were never seen again. We assume they fell into it and drowned."

"What about Captain Briggs, his wife and Sophia?" Aubrey asked.

"For a few weeks they seemed happy to continue living in the palace. But one night they disappeared from their room. We had no idea where they had gone, so search parties were sent out. After three days a pilot from the Albatross air force spotted Sophia wandering along the beach about ten kilometres to the east of Brusdor. The poor child was exhausted, and there was no sign of her parents. We brought her back and she was looked after by Godfrey the Giant Tortoise and his wife Grace. Godfrey went on to become her teacher."

Walli felt sorry for Sophia. "Did her parents ever reappear?"

"No. We think they might have rowed out to sea in the boat they arrived in, as it had disappeared from the beach. Perhaps they were looking for the *Mary Celeste*, although of course Animaux had moved many times since they arrived. They can't have known that, but they would have had no chance of finding their ship. Why they didn't take Sophia with them is a mystery, although it was stormy that night. Perhaps they thought the journey was too dangerous for her, and she would be safer on Animaux. It's a good job the albatross spotted her."

Tears welling in her eyes, Walli asked, "What happened to Sophia?"

Elizabeth was also starting to become emotional. "She was such a lovely girl. Very beautiful and clever. And with a kind heart. Sophia studied hard in school, and when she grew up she became a very talented artist. All of her paintings hang in the palace ballroom to this day. And she became very interested in gardening. I think Sophia had a happy life. She lived to the age of eighty-two and is buried in front of her favourite tree in the palace burial ground. It was a great honour, because only former presidents are buried there."

"What an incredible story," said Clifford, his voice wobbling.

Aubrey agreed. "You're right. And I never knew that Godfrey once had a wife. Elizabeth, what happened to her?"

"She passed away thirty years ago, when she was one hundred and forty. Such a young age for a giant tortoise."

Now it was Aubrey's turn to become weepy. "Poor Grace. And poor Godfrey."

The sombre mood was broken by Craig the Carrier Pigeon, who flew in through the window and landed on the floor in front of Elizabeth. "Madam President, I am sorry to interrupt, but we have the results of the competition." He removed a small canister tied to his leg and pulled out and unfolded a note that was inside it. "Here they are, together with an update on important news stories."

Elizabeth studied the note then addressed them all. "The suggestions for dealing with the plastic are as follows: Ignore it. Eat it. Each creature should take a little home, to make into an attractive object or bury it in their gardens. Bury it in the Deadly Bottomless Swamp. Put it in Aubrey's house and garden." She looked up. "The last idea was suggested by someone called Rick Rat. Does he mean *your* garden, Aubrey?"

"Yes, and it's not funny. Rick is not a good friend. I suppose this is his idea of a joke."

Elizabeth read some more. "It may interest you to know that Rick Rat started a collection in Wincot three days ago, called Save the Creatures of Animaux. He persuaded many creatures to give him money to help pay for the plastic clean-up. He has since disappeared with the money and the Crow police are trying to find him. He's clearly a very dishonest creature."

Walli had an idea. "Elizabeth, do you think the Weird Sisters might be able to help? Perhaps they could cast a spell to make the plastic vanish?"

"A good suggestion, Walli, but we've already tried it. The Sisters said they would use their magic, but only after receiving a very large payment. I persuaded Princess Crumble to give them three of her diamond tiaras. The Sisters accepted them, but then we found that none of their spells worked on plastic. However, they refused to give the tiaras back." Elizabeth returned her attention to the note. "What's this suggestion? My goodness, what a very good idea! Fatima Fox Cub has suggested that the plastic should be dropped into the volcano on Petits Animaux. Of course! That will destroy it, and will mean that none needs to be stored on the main island."

She turned to her chief scientists. "Is it possible to drop the plastic in the volcano?"

Bernyce answered first. "In theory, yes. Although it will take an enormous, coordinated effort. We can have teams of creatures take the plastic from the water and then have teams of others fly or swim with it across to Petits Animaux so it can be dumped in the volcano."

Orlando looked thoughtful. "We only need to clear the plastic from around the water inlets. When they are free, we can turn on the linear motor and move the island to a place where there is no plastic rubbish patch. We can continue to clear the waste from the beaches after that."

Elizabeth turned to Carinus. "Can you organise all the necessary resources? This is the biggest mobilisation of creatures that Animaux has ever experienced, and it will need to be carefully managed."

"It will be done, Madam President. You can rely on me, plus all your fellow citizens."

After receiving Elizabeth's permission, Carinus left the room and began to work with his senior team, plus the Animaux army, navy and air forces, to tackle the problem.

Clifford told the chief scientists that he would prepare a list of the locations of all the floating rubbish patches he was aware of, so that Animaux would never land in one again. Elizabeth ended the meeting, giving Aubrey his coveted selfie and telling Walli how much she liked her hat.

Over the next two weeks, most of the population of Animaux went to the coast and helped with the clean-up. It was a gigantic effort. The animals collected many hundreds of tonnes of plastic and took it to Petits Animaux to be destroyed. Acrid black smoke poured from the cone of the volcano as the plastic was incinerated, replacing the usual yellow-brown smoke.

Finally, after much hard work, the job was done. The water inlets were unblocked, the motor fired up, and Animaux swiftly moved away from the plastic patch to calmer waters and a welcoming sea of green.

The arrival of humans from the *Mary Celeste* one hundred and forty years before was the first time the species had an impact on Animaux. The arrival of the plastic was the second time. And trouble always comes in threes.

Scene Three – And So To Bed

Aubrey, Clifford and Walli had helped with the plastic clearance at Cedilla on Sea. When their work was over, it was time to return home. They were so tired that they hardly spoke on the train journey back to Wincot, nor as they trundled slowly on the skateboard up Fluffy Cloud Lane.

It was 10pm by the time they walked into Aubrey's house.

The turkey yawned. "Let's go to bed. I feel I could sleep for days! We can discuss our plastic adventure tomorrow, after we've had a good rest."

The friends wished each other sweet dreams and went up the stairs. As soon as they were in bed, they fell into a deep sleep: the kind of sleep reserved for good creatures that have done really important things.

*

The noise woke them. They all sat up, wondering where it had come from. Clifford and Walli left their room and found Aubrey in the hallway.

"Did you hear that?" he asked. "It wasn't me this time. I'm not playing the Black Skullanthemum trick again, I promise. I think there's a creature downstairs."

The friends listened intently, their hearts thumping.

Suddenly there was a cry of anguish from the ground floor, and they clung together in fear.

And then the creature called out. "Mummy, Mummy, where are you? I don't know where I am. I'm scared, Mummy!"

It had been one hundred and forty years since Sophia Briggs had arrived on Animaux.

And now it was Daisy Ansell's turn.

COMING SOON

Aubrey, Clifford and Walli will be back soon with more adventures. Please keep your eyes open for 'Who's There?' and four other tales. For the latest news, continue to check out milomcgivern.com.

This book is printed on paper from sustainable sources managed under the Forest Stewardship Council (FSC) scheme.

It has been printed in the UK to reduce transportation miles and their impact upon the environment.

For every new title that Troubador publishes, we plant a tree to offset CO_2, partnering with the More Trees scheme.

For more about how Troubador offsets its environmental impact, see www.troubador.co.uk/about/